MW00527667

A
CHRISTMAS
GHOST
STORY

A CHRISTMAS GHOST STORY

KIM NEWMAN

TITAN BOOKS

A Christmas Ghost Story
Print edition ISBN: 9781835410691
Signed edition ISBN: 9781835411957
E-book edition ISBN: 9781835410660

Published by Titan Books
A division of Titan Publishing Group Ltd
144 Southwark Street, London SE1 0UP
www.titanbooks.com

First edition: October 2024
10 9 8 7 6 5 4 3 2 1

A CIP catalogue record for this title is available from the British Library.

Printed and bound by
CPI Group (UK) Ltd, Croydon CR0 4YY

For Lydia

*'The following programme is not suitable for those of a
nervous disposition or children who should be in their beds…'*

DECEMBER THE FIRST.

Half past two in the afternoon.

THE SOMERSET LEVELS. Greyer than green.

Rust cycled along the A road from the County Town. Hours before dusk, he had his lights on.

Low, heavy cloud. Standing pools in flat fields. Brimming ditches.

Three years ago, the levels flooded over the holidays. The Six Elms Cut-Off became impassable. Rust and his mother survived till January on Christmas tree chocs and back-of-the-larder tins. Mum kept saying 'mustn't grumble, there's a war on'. He didn't get the joke. The council said it couldn't happen again. Rust didn't trust the council to tell the truth about extreme weather events. The Knell of Doom podcast had more credibility. Their advice for his postcode was 'buy a boat'.

His bicycle wheels cut a line through mud-film on the road. His face pushed into spits. The aerodynamic Gargantuabot

Rex helmet protected his ears. This wasn't proper rain. Just water in the air.

He was cycling through the Next Village Over when the Christmas Wars kicked off.

A thousand and one lights came on.

It had started with the first house past the village sign. They initiated hostilities years before the flood. Officially, their look was Traditional Christmas. More lighting effects than stadium rock. Fairy lights around every window and strangling every bush. Basically, Bling Christmas.

From a bed of artificial snow, a plaster golem with million-watt LED eyes surveyed the battlefront. Its white football head swivelled like a security camera. Fixed to the roof with hurricane-resistant wire, the Amazing Colossal Father Christmas sat atop a sleigh pulled by reindeer *kaiju*. A 'ho ho ho' loop would play until Twelfth Night…

At first, the rest of the village got up a petition to shut down the display.

When that only made the aggressor add more lights, they returned fire. The fad went viral. Neighbours would literally not be outshone.

The house across the road declared Vegas Christmas. Bigger, brighter, more blaring. Neon tubes and audio loops of snippets from *Sinatra Sings Swinging Carols* or whatever the Rat Pack Christmas album was called. Mum had it on vinyl. Mob boss Santa with eyes like angry ball bearings glared across the road at the snow sentinel. Vegas deer wore shades and packed heat.

It didn't stop there.

All through the village, systems came to life. Rust cycled down the road, veering as if dodging shellfire. Some displays would require age verification if they were websites. Rust had learned how to seem over eighteen online before he was twelve. He wasn't shocked by Porn Christmas (mooning Santa, sexy girl elves, obscene gnomes) or Horror Christmas (axe-wielding Saint Nick, zombie reindeer, ghost snowman).

It was a good thing afternoon traffic was light or there'd be nasty accidents. Every year, bedazzled passers-through drove into the ditch by the Coaching Inn. In the snug, Garage Gary waited for accidents like the wreckers who lured ships on the rocks. Mum would hire a horse and haul her car ten miles to Yeovil for servicing to avoid being plundered by Garage Gary.

The wars had gone on too long and cost too much time, money and mental strain... but the village collectively went even more nuts and stuck at it no matter what the council, the fire safety officer or a few clergymen said. Now Rust had seen it, he'd avoid cycling this way until February.

At the Y-fork past the Coaching Inn, he turned off the A road onto the B road – the only way into Sutton Mallet. The B road wasn't gritted. Low-hanging branches weren't trimmed.

He slowed a little, running low on puff.

'Gargantuabots, go go go,' he said.

The battle call spurred him on.

Sutton Mallet didn't hold with the Christmas Wars. A bare minimum of decorations was their policy. Holly and mistletoe. Plain lights. Season's Greetings. Nothing to attract attention.

The Next Village Over got on local news every year. Mr Bling would be interviewed, neighbours fuming in the background. A vicar would express qualified approval. ITV West would blur images behind Mr Porn and Miss Horror. Uncensored footage would be on the net by midnight.

Three minutes on local news was what it was all about. Highlight of the year.

Not for Sutton Mallet. They didn't want to be on local news. Or national. Or live-streamed. Or bothered at all.

They'd had too much of that, thank you very much.

Sutton Mallet wasn't overly keen on Rust's Paraphenomenon Pod either. Expressions like 'most haunted village in England' provoked overly cheerful suggestions he should get outdoors in the fresh air – hah! – and not let his eyes go googly staring at screens all the time. *He be daft to put credit in old spook tales. If ghosties there be, best they be left to thesselves, my lover, eh?*

Even at wheezing speed, Rust shot through Sutton Mallet inside a minute. Houses (not many), church, tiny triangular green, pillar box... then more B road and almost total dark. No street lighting on the levels.

A reflective roadside sign flashed 'Cats Eyes Removed'.

Mum said it was a service offered at Daintry Farm, along with 'Fresh Eggs and Corn Dollies'. Rust never believed her. They didn't have cats at Six Elms, so they'd no need for eye removals.

There was a water bowl at home with the name 'Fillip' glazed in the rim. Mum clammed up when asked about it, still not over a trauma forty-plus years later. Rust didn't know whether Fillip had been a cat or a dog or a whatever. Had it really been called Fillip – a boost or stimulus – or had Little Angie not known how to spell Philip? She still couldn't spell a lot of words, which ought to be an issue for an author. Mum said she thought ahead too fast to look up spellings or quibble about whiches and thats. The computer fixed any mistakes. She didn't get that a sub-routine of her word processing program did the spell-check, not the computer – which was just a box. She also wasn't into having it explained to her for the umpty-fifth time.

Fillip remained a mystery. Even Nana in Germany changed the subject if it came up. Still, there was no enthusiasm for throwing out the dry bowl or even shoving it at the back of a cupboard. At Christmas, the bowl had a ritual use.

Six Elms wasn't in Sutton Mallet but a mile and a half beyond the village at the end of the Cut-Off. The Cut-Off wasn't even a C road – more a C minus, with a scribbled 'could do better if it tried'. The three-hundred-yard obstacle course could be cycled or walked by the brave, but only two motor vehicles were nippy enough to negotiate each dip and swerve. One was Mum's not remotely new Hatch Mini. The other was the Milk Float, an electric Royal Mail post-van. Post-Lady Petal cheerfully delivered to the farthest outposts of civilisation.

Coming up to the Cut-Off, Rust saw orange lights wobbling through the gloom and heard a *zzzhh* sound. The sort of phenomenon misdiagnosed as para by normies. He recognised the roof-rim lights of the Milk Float.

The van slid out of Six Elms Cut-Off as Rust reached the turning. Its horn parped 'pa-rum-pa-pum-pum' at him. A December option. The usual honk was 'cu-cu-cucu-ra-cha'.

He leaned his bike backwards so the Milk Float could pass without squashing him. The driver wasn't Post-Lady Petal. Rust had the impression of a face under a cap. A white face. Petal was Jamaican. Leaning into the verge meant brushing wet shrubbery. This side of Sutton Mallet, roads were hemmed by hedges rather than ditches. Twigs scraped his helmet.

The Milk Float's rear lights receded. Not a UFO. An IDO – Identified Driven Object. Squinting at pulsing orange bars and blobs, he understood how a mistaken normie could call a paraphenomenon tip-line and waste the time of serious researchers. The electric *zzzhh* was like a sci-fi sound effect.

Stopping was a mistake. He was suddenly very cold. One final push – the trickiest stretch – and he'd be home to save Christmas.

He could give up and trundle-walk to Six Elms.

Not today. He was out in the fresh air – hah! He'd cycled through the zone of drizzle. He took a deep breath. Ice-drops stung his alveoli. They'd done alveoli – little nobbles inside your lungs – in Bio. Mum called them oliveoili. It was sometimes hard to believe she had a teaching qualification.

He skid turned into the Cut-Off.

Angie should have prioritised clearing the mantelpiece in the sitting room. For the cards. But she procrastinated, ticking off less-fraught items. Always the mantel was in the back of her mind.

They'd put up the lights last night, intent on a before-dawn switch-on… but that plan went south.

Russell was out of the way, fetching a vital component from the Electrical Outlet in the County Town. The once-failing shop had been saved by a Christmas miracle in the form of the Next Village Over's insatiable demand for lights, adaptors, cables, control systems and suitcase-sized atomic piles.

This afternoon, she dug out pre-industrial Christmas decorations from under the stairs. A few surviving glass baubles from her childhood nestled in a carton which smelled of tennis balls forty-five years after they were lost in long grass.

She found the stiff, gold-spackled wicker wreath she'd made sixteen years ago while pregnant. Never mind the Christ child, she had her own baby on the way and felt compelled to weave a garland. She put the wreath up on her office door.

Some decorations dated back to her parents' OG austerity childhoods. They'd come out of the cupboard every year since Wickingses came to Six Elms, before she was born. Dad's sturdy wooden soldiers would be parade-ready long after Russell's last breakable plastic Gargantuabot was slagged.

Decorating on December the First was a Dad thing. Mum couldn't get enthusiastic until school broke up and carol concerts were out of the way. Her parents were both teachers but Dad was Science and didn't have to worry about carol concerts. Mum was Music, so rowing with tone-deaf parents and tin-eared choristers consumed her afternoons and spilled into her evenings from five minutes past Guy Fawkes Night till the end of term. Mum didn't think of carol concerts as Christmas treats, but a black mark on the calendar which had to be got past before she could make mince pies with too much mince or wrap this year's presents with last year's paper.

Dad and Angie would already have been through the double issues of the *Radio* and *TV Times* with highlighter pens, flagging conflicts of interest. Mum's word on disputes was final. Even Dad – missing the racing so Angie could watch *Miss Marple* – had to admit her rulings were fair. Still, Angie was once denied the final episode of a *Doctor Who* so Dad could see a space shuttle take-off. She'd made him buy her the video of that exact serial when it came out on cassette twelve years later and she was away at uni without a player to watch it on. Video recorders ended the era of scheduling disputes, but came along after the quality of Christmas telly fell off a cliff and it was impossible to find one programme worth watching let alone two on at the same time.

Angie checked supplies and found enough wrapping paper, sticky tape and gift tags for another year. She'd overbought after the flood. Overbuying was a Wickings thing – except, obviously, when it came to vital components. She should have told Russell to buy three or four assorted doodads. She was bound to have missed something essential when collecting his big present – a digital camera and assorted peripherals – and it would be a job to get the set-up working by Boxing Day.

Her technical knowledge had juddered to a halt in the 1990s. She was lucky to have a fifteen-year-old tech wizard in residence to look at her like an idiot because she didn't know the difference between SCART, USB and the RSPB. Russell didn't believe that when Angie was his age she'd asked for – and received and *used* – a soldering iron for Christmas. She still had the wiring diagrams she and Dad had devised, but the gadgets they'd made were long gone – probably chucked out when they didn't work. It gave her a tiny little thrill that for all his digiskillz – and he complained about *her* spelling – he looked at a soldering iron as if it were a Pictish relic. Thanks to his archaeology craze, he'd have more idea how to use a Pictish relic.

Angie marked Russell's childhood through craze phases.

First and worst was the Schloup, the obsession of Russell's toddlerhood. *Sunil and the Schloup* used to be on every Christmas when Tony Blair was Prime Minister (not that there was a connection she knew of). The cartoon was unbearable to adults, which might have been the appeal for kids. The Schloup was a shape-changing silver alien or ectoplasmic entity. Mostly, it looked like a puddle with eyes. Russell owned three major schloups (Mange, Plop and Wilberforce) and a jarful of melted minischloups from packets of Sugar Puffs. He filled in schloup colouring books meticulously, never crayoning over the lines. A schloup bobble-hat was worn everywhere including the bath and bed until it was tragically lost at sea.

For nearly two years, the excruciating 'The Schloup Schloup Song' was on repeat in Six Elms House. In the dark hours she heard it start up again and reflected on her life choices. Maybe conceiving a new Wickings wasn't her best idea. Then Russell made her 'schloup soup' breakfast – a runny omelette with squashed tomato eyes – and she disowned her night thoughts as whispers of the Devil and throbbed with a soppiness she'd deny under oath. A decade on, the song still made her retch then go misty-eyed whenever it featured on a Worst Singles of All Time playlist.

When Russell was five, a meteor ripped the skies of Schloupworld and triggered an extinction-level event. The Age of the Schloup ended. Mange was got rid of when corroded batteries went toxic, Plop burst and Wilberforce – the favourite – was put in a bin only to be surreptitiously rescued and stored. A time would come when Russell would wish he still had useless things from his childhood. She'd give a lot to have back the non-functioning gadgets she and Dad made. Not to mention Fillip.

The new craze phase was Gargantuabots. Japanese robots who defended the Earth from monster threats. The plot of the cartoon was as complex as all of Shakespeare's history plays run one after the other. Gargantuabots toys – no, sorry, *figures* – had a fixed hierarchy. Also vital were games, comics, books, stickers and bubble-bath. She'd seen the live-action *Gargantuabots Go Go Go* more times in the cinema and on DVD than her own favourite movie – *Body Heat*, which opened up 'sexy suspense' to her when she was twelve. Janet Speke showed her the video to prove she was allowed to rent an '18 certificate' tape. It turned out she wasn't – her older sister Juliet took it out of Valerie's Videos for her. Kathleen Turner, star of *Body Heat*, was the voice of Gretelgeuse, commander of monster threats in *Gargantuabots Go Go Go*. Angie reckoned their destinies were entwined. She hoped to get Kathleen Turner to narrate the Angelica Wickings audiobook library.

The craze never completely ended. Russell was a purist who could lecture for hours on the superiority of earlier iterations of the franchise. Gargantuabots (Second Series) – never to be confused with the second season of *Gargantuabots: The Series* – was the apogee of perfection. Angie was not going to disagree. Russell despised *Botz Boyz*, the current reboot, the way established churches loathed popular heresies. He binged the webtoon in secret on his tablet and swapped het-up posts with an online community of like-minded botbros. His Gargantuabots (Second Series) cadre remained in their prime position on the mantelpiece in the sitting room for eleven months of the year.

She mustn't put it off much longer. A thing that must be done. Or was it a thing which must be done?

The cadre must give way to the cards.

After Gargantuabots came archaeology. Russell didn't get that from a cartoon but from Daniel, who came to the levels to investigate a site where some well-off-their-patch Vikings were buried after a spirited argument with Alfred the Great. Angie let out the spare room to Daniel for a summer. He eventually went north, following retreating Vikings and was in Sweden now, piecing together bits of longboat. The archaeology craze led to much digging on the property. Russell had a museum shelf of Six Elms finds – odd-shaped stones, nails, bits of clay pipe, animal bones and six glass marbles in a tobacco tin. He was keen on the idea of smashing the ugly concrete yard between gatepost and house. Mysteries might be buried beneath.

She approved of the archaeology craze – more than the Schloup and Gargantuabots, not just because it was less expensive. He was drawn into it by a person, not a glorified toy advert in cartoon form. The pursuit fit his character. Russell liked to do things properly, which often meant more slowly than was convenient. He had a horror of crayoning outside the lines. Grown-ups – including her, she admitted – thought it weird or somehow wrong. Daniel didn't. He let her son know his method was sound, even superior. He shouldn't be nagged into being ashamed of it. The example made her resolve to be more tolerant of Russell's neat and tidy ways. He was attentive to details.

She appreciated their parallel interests: she wrote mysteries, he dug for answers. Her way to a plot solution and his to a find were very alike. Much careful spadework, then a big ta-daa reveal. Slow-slow-*quick*. It must be inherited.

Archaeology, however, led to paraphenomena. On which she was less keen.

Living near Sutton Mallet made her wary of spook stuff.

Cursed objects. Hauntings. Apparitions. Manifestations. Encounters. More letters she didn't understand. She knew ESP from *The X-Files* but needed to have EVP explained to her. A tenet of sexy suspense was that mysteries should have rational solutions. It couldn't be ghosts. Or aliens. It had to be a scheming husband after the inheritance or a long-dumped boyfriend who'd never stopped obsessing. *Warlock Wendy*, the one time she'd coloured outside that line, was her big flop.

Russell couldn't see why paraphenomenal explanations weren't rational. He wanted ghosts to be real but still more wanted them to be *understood*. It wasn't superstition, it was unknown science. He sought para-explanations and good luck to him. His listeners were into the weird and witchy. Her readers would call her a cheat on Goodreads if she went that way again. She kept to scheming husbands and bad boyfriends.

In his archaeology phase, Russell dug in the earth – so carefully he never came home dirty. Now he dug on the internet. Angie tried not to have slow-release panic attacks about it. A few odd fringy followers prompted her to disable comments on her own site. She hadn't a clue how to impose limits on her son's online activity and was against censorious parenting on principle. Smut was the least of it. She'd done a lot of research – well, she'd talked with people who'd done a lot of research – on web-dangers for *Samantha Stalked*. Now, what she knew terrified her as much as what she didn't.

Paraphenomena on the net was fringe of fringe. Way out and whacky. The Weirdo Zone. She couldn't persuade Russell to disable comments on his podcast and sometimes scanned public messages to him – many from his arch-rivals the Peason Twins – with horror. She knew about doxxing, swatting, DDS, deepfakes, cancellation, ransomware, pile-ons and digibombs, even if Russell poked holes in the ways Samantha's stalker used them. Since she wrote the book, all of two years ago, new techniques of doing harm over the internet had been invented.

She imagined her son alone on the shore of a sea of black ink twinkling with reflected lights from wicked stars. Vast malignities moved in the deep dark. Maybe they were what schloups grew up to be.

Or perhaps she was just still afraid of ghost stories.

A CHRISTMAS GHOST STORY
'THE CARDS'

From the story by Sir Harcourt Mountmain.
Starring Leslie Veneer as 'Marshalsea Rooke'.

A bleak December landscape. The snow cover isn't soft delight, but hard-packed and grit-specked. A black, leafless tree at a crossroads. An earth-brown path across white ground. Only boots have trudged here. No wheel-ruts.

A ragged man walks. He wears a three-cornered hat. Two tatty coats bulk him out but don't keep him warm. A red scarf winds round his face. Apart from the brown mud and red scarf, this is a black-and-white picture. Smudges of colour don't indicate cheer.

The ragged man has a sack slung over his back. He turns left by the tree, taking the road less trudged. He makes new footprints. His boots are inadequate. He'll be lucky not to keep Christmas by losing a toe.

He comes to a hollow and looks at a sign. Wychward Cottage. There seems to be no dwelling – just a hillock of snow. But a sunken path leads to the hump. Snarl-faces stick out of snow-banks. Carved wood-imps. Their eyes are frozen berries. The sack-carrier warily treads the path.

This is Wychward Cottage. Drifts slope up almost to the tops of the windows. A way to a front door is clear. A twist of iron in the shape of a pentacle hangs from the lintel. On the door is a wreath – an angry moonface of old hard bread, cheeks full but scowling, laurel and oleander leaves for a fringe and forkbeard.

The ragged man unshoulders his sack and clangs the pentacle.

Snow falls away from a window. A circular motion inside makes a hole in frosted glass. An unhealthy eye peers through. The door opens and the ragged man steps back.

The resident – Marshalsea Rooke – is a head shorter than his caller, stout as a pudding. Buttons burst off his waistcoat, sewn-up rips down his britches seams. Rooke has a bald pate. His side-whiskers are teased out to twirlable points. His lapels are embroidered with stars, runes, hexes and numbers. His cravat is violently purple, an unnatural colour.

The ragged man takes a packet from his sack. He doesn't like to hold it. Rooke's bony hand sticks out. The packet drops on a mat. The caller touches his hat-brim and scarpers, not stopping for breath until he's off the property.

Rooke looks down. The envelope creeps towards his long-toed shoe. He speaks...

A Merry Christimas to you too, my little
horribles.

He stamps on the squirming envelope. It
squelches and crunches.

∼

After the dips and swerves of the Cut-Off, Rust came to the
gateless gatepost. Perched on top was a scale model of Six
Elms House. Not a bird-table, but an American-style mailbox.
Mum had gone out with Artisanal Eric, the mailbox maker,
for a while. She'd ghosted him after a row about Brexit. The
wood-turner was in favour because he worried about being
undercut by Poles. Eric made a neat mailbox, though.

A raised flag signified post delivered. Rust opened the hinged
front and took out a rubber-banded bundle. He trundled his
bike to the lean-to. While he was away, Mum had stuck felt
antlers to the Hatch Mini.

December the First was her day for the decorations.

It was tradition.

Wickings Christmas had many traditions, though they
weren't all traditional. The local news vicar who gave the Next
Village Over's sparklage a grudging pass would be less tolerant
of 'Christmas Cruels' – rude, wicked or silly versions of carols
Mum and Rust competed to make more offensive every year.
'Away in a Mangler', 'The Fight Before Christmas', 'The
Worst Noel'.

Putting rotten broken biscuit bits in Fillip's bowl on Christmas
Eve wasn't exactly giving or charitable. The plan was to make
the reindeer sick so Santa wouldn't get to Janet Speke's house
in High Ham. Mum kept that tradition even though her

school best friend/enemy had grown up and left High Ham ages back. Rust had never met Janet Speke, though she got mentioned *a lot*.

He crossed the forecourt to Six Elms House.

There hadn't been elms on the property since Dutch elm disease, which devastated the land when Mum was a little girl. The house was patchwork. It had partially fallen down several times, well before Wickingses came to Somerset. Successive owners built on or knocked down whatever they needed or felt like. No three windows matched. The roof was recent red tile. Grandad's attempt to restore the original thatch failed when muddy mould set in.

The forecourt was an uneven concrete wasteland Mum often said she'd like to take a hammer to. Rust would be happy to help her. Firewood was stacked under a tarpaulin which made frequent escape attempts; the lightest breeze would uproot the skewers of its guy-ropes as if a force ten weather event were sweeping the levels. The cultivated-in-summer garden was round the back, sheltered by the glass-ceilinged extension Mum used as an office. The out-buildings – two barns and a shed – had planning permission for remodelling as small lets. When Mum became Queen of Self-Published Suspense, she put her scheme to turn Six Elms into a profitable B&B on hold.

The shed was handy for keeping boxes of unsold Angelica Wickings books dry. One barn had power. It would do for a studio when the Paraphenomenon Pod pivoted to video in the New Year – if hints about the kit he wanted for his big present paid off. *Mistress Murder*, Mum's first book, was being made as a TV series in Poland, so she was in funds. Mum sold better in Polish than English – her translator Jerzy was up on spellings and the that/which conundrum. She'd eventually break the

ghosting to send Eric a gloat-mail about her Polish sales. She
was e-flirting with Jerzy, which would make it worse. Eric
lived in High Ham, so he might have an empty stocking on
Christmas morning too. Mum wasn't one to let things go.

The oldest part of Six Elms House was a flight of three
broad smooth steps up to the front door. Either side of the
steps were crouching stones – not tall enough to be called
standing, too solid to be dismissed as leaning. Household
wards blessed centuries earlier by wise women to deter Sutton
Mallet boggarts and bogeys from lolloping down the Cut-Off
to benight the good folk of Six Elms... or else dumped where
they were after being dug up in 1952 to make way for the
pool of concrete because they were too awkward to be hauled
anywhere else.

Either way, the crouching stones were a significant feature.
A tiny bit paraphen.

When he was small, Mum taught him to rap on the right
stone's noggin twice for luck on leaving the house and stroke
the left stone's nubbin three times for fortune coming back in.
He only broke the habit when he grew so tall he'd have to bend
down to touch the stones.

He let himself in.

∽

Christmas Control was the kitchen-dining room. It had been
two rooms before Angie's dad decided to play high-stakes
Jenga by taking out a wall. A column in the middle of the
room kept the rest of the house from falling on the big table.
The combination noticeboard, totem pole and essentials rack
was studded with hooks – Angie had replaced Dad's rusty nails

a few years ago, after Russell's tetanus scare – for items like scissors, torches, keys, the radiator bleed doodad (without it they'd freeze), and emergency burner phone (don't ask). Useful things were inclined to go for a wander.

The post also served as a demarcation point between cooking area and eating table.

A zoo of marzipanimals was laid out on a board. Christmas cookie ingredients were bought. Mince pies with too much mince were in the oven. Angie wasn't being flooded out of treats again. Space was cleared in the fridge for the turkey. That gap would fill and need to be cleared again before the bird arrived on the eighteenth – but she'd declared intent.

Christmas Central was the sitting room. The enormoscreen was overshadowed by a ceiling-scraping, heavily decorated tree. This year's pine was settled in the old tub. Strings of lights wound from the tree up into the eaves and out into the hall and beyond. Six Elms should be a constellation of lights, visible from Glastonbury Tor. She'd drawn diagrams. Russell had clambered up ladders, onto the roof, into crannies and through the attic to string the illuminations. The planned pre-dawn light-up was thwarted because a vital component was missing. It used to be a lack of batteries which ruined Christmas. Now, it was the want of a lead.

A shoebox of cables was on the low table, untangled and sorted through. They had every type but the right type, apparently. Russell had set aside three obsolete leads for binning – their blocky extrusions no longer fit the slimmer sockets on modern-day kit. She wasn't sure she wanted to chuck anything. It'd been a pain replacing the record player – the turntable, Russell called it – she'd thrown out after buying a now-sneered-at CD stack, but vinyl was back. Who knows which dead formats would eventually return and require cables? She still had her cassette tape of *Body Heat*, though the whole score – and hours more similar inspirational music – was programmed as a Spotify 'writing sexy suspense' playlist.

Facing the picture window was the little Victorian desk where she'd written *Mistress Murder*. On the desk was an advent calendar. The shiny illustration, as-yet unbroken by window-opening, showed an old-fashioned Christmas tree. Behind each window nestled a delicious chocolate. No Lego Gargantuabots this year. Just soft centres. Perhaps liqueurs for the last few days before the double-sized window on Christmas Eve. There'd better be a divisible-into-two-bites praline nut cluster in the crib behind the '24' window or Angie would lodge a complaint with the County Stores.

Then there was the mantelpiece.

The Gargantuabots (Second Series) cadre occupied the shelf beneath the framed poster of a woman in an evening gown, pulling a knife from her garter-sheath. She wore a 'Queen of Suspense' sash. Inset were the covers of the first three Angelica Wickings mysteries: *Mistress Murder*, *Warlock Wendy* and *Samantha Stalked*. Since then, she'd written *Honey Homicide* – Russell said it was a swizz since homicide and murder meant the same thing, which they didn't legally – and the format-stretching, better-reviewed if slower-selling *Heidi Whose Husband Killed Her*. Spoiler – Heidi wasn't killed but the husband was: all was revealed on the last page.

Russell dusted the cadre as carefully (and often) as maidservants polished the silver in vintage country house whodunits. Not a laser-blaster out of place, not a carapace scratched, not a detachable drone-hand lost under the sofa. The hard-to-find Gargantuabot Mauve was in place between

Team Leader Takashi and Red Rudiger. The sitting room had been secure from monster threats ever since the cadre took this high ground.

She didn't like to touch the preciouses, but the time had come.

Cards on this mantel was Wickings tradition.

She reached out...

... and heard the front door shoved open.

'Mum, I've saved Christmas,' called Russell.

She jumped and put her hand in her pocket.

Her son clumped through the hallway and pushed into the sitting room.

He'd taken off his helmet. He held a slender box.

'The proper cable,' he said. 'Type C.'

It looked exactly like half a dozen cables they already had, but this one had a bibble where they all had a bobble. She let him fit the lead between the bought-last-week bit of kit which controlled the lights and the adaptor which plugged into the mains. A blue light winked on a black box the size of a cigarette packet then turned white. This was what everyone wanted. OK for Go.

Russell took his tablet from a charging cradle and swiped, bringing up a menu.

He handed the tablet to her. He'd put a big red button in the middle of the screen.

'Press or wipe?' she asked.

Russell suppressed his Mum-you're-an-idiot look and patiently told her, 'Just touch. You know, like a button.'

'I'm familiar with the technology.'

She pressed the screen.

The Christmas tree sparkled to life. Electric candles burned in the corners of the room. Quiet tinkling accompanied the magic – distant sleigh-bells. Lights in sequence lit up throughout the house and outside. Russell had wired in a waving snowman, shooting star and baaahing flocks. A premium display. Old Wickings decorations. New Russell doodads. A complete seasonal ecosystem of electric cheer and damn the smart meter.

Angie was slightly emotional. Not to a hugging degree.

The Gargantuabots hadn't lit up. Time for their annual holiday in cardboard.

'Christmas Wars have kicked off Next Village Over,' Russell reported.

'We are non-combatants, Russell,' she reminded him.

'Rust,' he insisted, automatically.

'Rust,' she corrected herself – promising she'd not deadname him again, knowing she would. 'There were Christmas lights at Six Elms well before insanity took hold Next Village Over and you invented an app to control our display.'

'Coded,' he autocorrected.

'Coded an app. Going large on decorations has been a Wickings tradition since the year dot… along with mince pies with too much mince… denial of Santa service to Janet Speke in High Ham… wrapping this year's present to you in the paper you wrapped last year's present to me in… the wonky angel Mum made with toilet roll tubes and silver paper while tipsy on sherry…'

Fillip's bowl was still by the sink in the kitchen, ready for rotten broken biscuit bits.

More happily, Mum's wonky angel – the Angie Gabrielle, she called it, though Angie's middle name was Gudrun – was on top of the tree, wings underlit by Russell's – *Rust's* – magic stars.

'… and cards in a row on the mantelpiece.'

Not the Gargantuabots (Second Series) cadre.

For a moment, peerless paraphenomenal investigator Rust looked like wobbly-underlipped Russell when someone crayoned outside a line.

Knowing better than to let Angie break or lose something even more vital than a Type C lead, Russell fetched a box and effected an evacuation of the cadre. He took as much care as if he were delivering babies. He lingered longer with Mauve than the others. He was less keen on Red Rudiger, who turned out to be a double agent for Gretelgeuse in the fourth season.

On Twelfth Night, the button would be unpressed and the decorations dismantled. Then Gargantuabots would return to their post. How many years would it be before Russell left his collectables in storage past January the Sixth? If the market held up and he put the complete cadre on eBay in three years' time, her son wouldn't need a student loan. Mauve alone would support him for two terms.

He took the box into the hall. Angie followed. One major player to bring onto the pitch. Russell stood, reluctant to consign the cadre to darkness.

'Garglebaskets guard our hearth eleven months of the year,' she said. 'Then make way for cards. Tradition.'

'Hearth-wards *are* a common practice,' admitted Russell, putting the box away in the cupboard under the stairs. 'I did a Paraphenomenon Pod about them.'

'Robots made in Japan can protect a house in Somerset from spooks?'

'If you believe hard enough. You know, like you do in Christmas. We have more traditional wards.'

Russell hauled open the front door. Electric starlight fell on the crouching stones.

She expected she'd told Russell stories about the stones he remembered better than she did. She made up so many stories they couldn't all stick in her head. She needed outside readers to point out when policemen changed names between chapters.

'Someone put the stones here for a reason,' said Russell.

'To scrape muddy boots?'

'Probably to ward off entities. From…'

He nodded in the direction of Sutton Mallet – 'the most haunted village in England', not that she'd ever seen or felt or smelled or sensed anything paraphenomenal around here… not unless you counted her wild imagination.

Russell shut the door. She'd worried his latest craze would bring back the nightmares he had when he was five but his interest was in science (well, parascience) not scariness. He was snooty about podcasters (like the Peason Twins) who sexed up their investigations with echoey voices and spooky sound effects. She noticed but didn't mention that shivery ghost merchants got more listens than him being sensible.

She rooted under the stairs and found what she needed.

'Much as we might want to ward off entities most of the year, we can't have psychic blocks on the chimney on Christmas Eve.'

She held Jolly Old Saint Nick – the oldest of the vintage Wickings decorations.

'Let's put him where he belongs.'

Inside Wychward Cottage, a low-ceilinged lair.

A miniature nativity scene has stuffed, costumed rats as Joseph, Mary and the kings. An oozing giant slug is pinned into a tiny manger. A festive blasphemy.

The room is cluttered with tomes, sky charts and witchy decor. Marshalsea Rooke might call himself a sorcerer but he's a warlock. He practises the blackest of black arts.

Rooke putters in. He drops a lettuce leaf to feed Baby Jesus. He places the squashed envelope on a bloodied butcher's block. He breaks the wax seal with a letter-opener and scrapes insect parts into a bowl.

Didn't have to be live scarabaeus beetles, Master Pothekar. As you knew well. A fancy fellow's idea of a joke on the old fool. Eh what, what hey? Well, some olderly fools be not so foolish... Ahem, he he, ah what… aha, the process is begun. Begun it be.

He crushes bug bits further with a mortar. A grimoire is propped open like a recipe book. Gruesome ingredients are prepared. A live goose is dissected and pinned open to expose palpitating organs. Its beak is clamped to prevent honking.

Rooke carves a pentagram into the thick icing of a bulging sac of pudding. A dry severed hand makes a V-sign. Candlewicks burn from its stuck-up fingertips.

In the middle of the room is a brick firepit. An iron grille covers hot coals. Rooke hefts the goose onto the grille.

Who's a pretty goosie? Such a fine plump bird. Reared for parson's table. No roast bird for the goodly Reverend Godly this year. Parson must make do with cold mutton. Privation is meat for the soul, saith the lesson. We shall see how the sermoniser likes such meat when it's his own soul being prived. A mite less joyously, I'll be bound. You'll serve my purpose better than you'd serve Godly's table. Mark my words and my word's my mark. Now it must be done in correct and proper order.

Rooke pours beetle-bits into the open wound, which widens like a mouth. Then he slips the pudding, pentagram side-up, into the gaping hole.

A sheep's stomach lining would have done, cording to Maistre Grossinger of Gratz. But the belly-sac of a baptised Christian child's best, cording to Magister Marshalsea Rooke of Rokesby Roylott. How the devout lad did fuss and skitter, Mistress Goose. Should have pinned his beak too. Still, 'twas worth all effort. Ha and ho. Yes and ready.

Rooke is satisfied with the pudding/goose, which begins to steam. He picks up the hand of glory.

Now, to summon the Spirit of Christimas…

The goose-pudding transforms like clay kneaded by invisible hands. It is shaped into an organic womb with a crusty Scotch-egg exterior. Rooke squirms in pleasure.

Be you welcome, Master Christimas.

The fingercandles flare. Blue light sparkles around the egg. It cracks. Pieces fall away, disclosing a yolky pillow. In this crib lies a cherub swaddled in ivy. The baby has an old man's beard and matching kiss-curl. Little feathery wings waggle. The cherub gurgles, merry and trusting. Rooke's brows knit. Malign purpose shows in his grimace.

T'has been done. A summonation! Behold, the Spirit of Christimas... the giving heart of a Christian child... the ancient power of a thrice-blooded feast!

Rooke puts out a long finger, which the cherub grasps in its pudgy hand.

Strong little summonation, aren't you? As to be expected. If you weren't a fit fat fellah, you'd be no goose supper at all. You lie there, Master Christimas. I've a gift for you. A season's present, like Christians give... a horsie or a spinning top.

Rooke picks up a sharp stake made of entwined holly sprigs. He pricks his finger to test the point. A ruby of blood swells and he flicks it away.

Now where would your generous heart be? Oh yes, in the chest, 'tween the lungs. Have to slide this up under the ribs. Now, Merry Christimas!

Rooke strikes down with the stake.

Not easy to penetrate the sternum, but it must be done. Done it must be. There, precious tyke, you've a sprig of holly through your heart. It is Magister Rooke who shall have the merriest of holidays, praise be to, ah, Diabolus.

At the moment of final satisfaction, Rooke is distracted. He looks away from the shrivelled thing he has sacrificed - it is resolving to

```
red ice crystals and stringy dough - to the
doormat, where another envelope lies.
```

Ah...

∽

They went back to the sitting room.

Angie hung Jolly Old Saint Nick from a branch just below the tree top. *Święty Mikołaj*, Jerzy called him – which she couldn't help but read as Sweaty McOladge. From his station, Sweaty McOladge could look up the raiment of the Wonky Angel. Her mother used to make out the pair were an item, but Angie didn't like the idea. He was Father Christmas, not Boyfriend Christmas. Dad suggested JOSN was Angie Gabrielle's bodyguard, which made sense. The Saint Nick ornament was from just after the War. He looked like a burly bloke who could take care of himself if Rommel invaded the North Pole.

It took a few moments to be satisfied with the placement.

'There, perfect,' Angie said. 'You understand the importance of ritual. I'm sure you can cast a pod about that. Folk belief. Family folk belief. Wickingses Wayses. You know what's next… today's advent calendar window – then the cards.'

Russell was less keen. Was this an aspect of Christmas – without the benefit of an app – he'd gone off? Every year, he scorned something once delightful as babyish. Stocking on the bedpost. Nuts and nectarines. The disappointing *Doctor Who* special. She'd been the same.

Angie and Russell rolled chairs to the desk. Russell wasn't impressed by the advent calendar picture. He couldn't open a window by swiping his tablet.

'It'll be a robin behind the first window,' she said. 'It always is.'

'It was Gargantuabot Rex last year.'

'We had a Garglebasket calendar from Japan then. We've gone trad this year. County Stores. No Lego, but chocolate…'

Russell scratched the window marked '1'. Angie tutted him into freezing.

'Cowboy, change your ways today…' she said. 'Examination of the envelopes first… then opening of the window and consumption of the treat… then opening of the cards.'

For all his *properly and slowly* habit, Russell was impatient. He got the chocolate on odd-numbered days.

'Do we have dead tree cards?' he asked. 'Surely no one sends them any more.'

'You brought in the post.'

Bundled with begging letters from charities and greetings from utility companies whose prices would be going up in the New Year were two envelopes with handwritten addresses.

'Two no ones here,' she said.

One envelope, addressed to Angelica and Russell, had Mum and Horst's address in Germany on the back. Mum and Horst organised and posted early for Christmas. The other envelope was a mystery.

'It's for you,' she told Russell.

Beside the Christmas stamp was a printed number '1', like on an advent calendar window. The card was addressed to

Master Russell Wickings,
Six Elms House,
nr Sutton Mallet, Somerset.

No postcode. Post-Lady Petal knew her route and could deliver to the most approximate or scrawled addresses. The writing wasn't illegible – a copperplate so perfect Angie couldn't tell if it was done longhand or cleverly printed.

Russell found his scalpel in a pot on the desk.

'Ritual, remember,' she said. 'Advent window, chocolate, then you open your card.'

'I don't know who it's from.'

'One of your followers?'

'It's probably a curse from the Peasons.'

He might be right. Perry and Skye Peason were evil mutants.

Russell performed a delicate slice on the tab of the first window and winkled out a small wrapped chocolate. He scraped off the foil, suddenly greedy.

'Hold your hosses,' she said, noticing 'slow and sure' got deprioritised at the whiff of a soft centre. 'What's the picture? Is it a robin?'

Russell peered at the illustration behind the flap of card.

'Can't tell,' he said. 'It's a smudge of red on white. Looks like a squashed cherry.'

She agreed with him. Weirdly abstract.

'A runover robin, perhaps,' she suggested.

'It's rubbish,' said Russell, popping the chocolate into his mouth.

'The naff is part of the magic,' she said.

'What's naff?' he asked, as if he had a pebble in his cheek.

'A posh way of saying rubbish. Popularised by Princess Di in the eighties.'

'Princess Who?'

He smirked, face still puffed out.

'Naff off,' she said. 'You be winding I up.'

'Gertcha... ach!'

He coughed.

'Pellet with poison?'

He choked, alarmingly. Angie realised he wasn't clowning. Then he stopped. The pebble was swallowed.

'I'm never eating another of those from this,' he said. 'You can give the odd chocs to the Tree Ghost.'

'Surprise liqueur? Catsick cordial?'

'Something hard – like a nut. Maybe a coffee bean. Or a seed. And off, like seriously off. You sure the calendar is this year's?'

He coughed again and licked the back of his hand. He couldn't get rid of the taste.

'And I've swallowed it so I'll die.'

'Can I have your presents?' she said. 'And the patent on your app. I'll be rich, I say, rich...'

He wasn't having any cheering-up.

'Goat, that was foul,' he said. 'Great Goat foul.'

Angie checked the back of the calendar for a date and couldn't find one. She looked again through the open window. That red smudge wasn't healthy. Had it changed shape, like a vengeful minischloup?

'I'm going to source affordable emetics,' he said, getting up.

'Not before you've opened your card.'

Russell sat down again. He was curious and had been thinking about it.

'I think I know who it's from,' he said. 'The vicar I recorded for the pod... with the poltergeist in the vestry.'

He scalpeled the envelope and slid out the card.

'Dead traditional, vicars,' he said. 'Even more than you. Look – here's your robin.'

He showed her the card.

A Victorian snow scene. Woodland at night. Star in the sky. Icing-thick drifts deep and crisp and even. A red-breasted robin on a bough. The bird wore a little red scarf.

Innocent, yet terrifying. She felt an icicle arrow in her chest.

Russell looked inside. He frowned.

'Funny, no signature. Just a rhyme.'

He got up and placed the card at the left end of the mantelpiece. '"Pinch-punch, first of the month",' she said, hearing a rasp in her voice.

He showed her the message. Yes…

PINCH-PUNCH, FIRST OF THE MONTH

'"And no return of any kind",' said Russell, turning to her. '*Not* very Christmassy.'

Angie made a sound in her throat, a squeak which might grow into a scream. It startled Russell.

She held her fists up to her cheeks.

'Mum, what is it? What's wrong?'

```
Rooke picks up the envelope, which is unsealed.
It unfolds of its own accord and the magister
sees a Christmas card. A robin on a branch in
a wood in winter. Snow all around.

He looks inside.

In a fine hand is written 'Pinch-punch, first
of the month...'

Rooke, perturbed, looks at the card as if it
were a little window into eternal night.
```

'...and no return of any kind.'

His gaze is drawn into the snowy woodland
picture - a fir forest, lit by a single star
in the black sky.

The robin turns and twitters, leaking blood.
Where blood drops, a tiny green shoot appears
out of the frozen earth.

Rooke puts the card on the mantelpiece. Wags
finger.

Fie and fee, can't affright me.

Rooke does not look away.

His mother irritated him to cold fury many times – and, quietly,
Rust knew he returned the favour – but had rarely scared him
before. She wasn't even trying. Mum was so terrified of – of
what? – she hadn't the bandwidth to think about anything else.
On a day when she was usually full of the joys of the season.

She shut up and retreated to her writing office. Without
explaining.

Rust pulled the mince pies with too much mince out of
the oven when the smoke alarm went off. They were now the
mince pies with too much charcoal.

The alarm didn't bring Mum into the kitchen. Which rang
other alarms.

When Mum was in her office, he had to forage for himself.
With the burned lids prised off, the pies were edible. He
scalded the roof of his mouth with molten mince.

Back in the sitting room, he re-examined the card that had set Mum off.

He couldn't see anything in it. No pirates' Black Spot.

There was no artist credit – no publishers' marks at all – but it didn't look home-made. The Peason Twins would be more obvious about trying to scare him. They'd send necromancer's runes or death notes. Probably not via snail mail. Perry and Skye wouldn't know how to stick a stamp on a letter. He only did because Mum preferred her birthday card in the post rather than propped on the breakfast table. Having commissioned the mailbox, she wanted something nice in it on special days. Not whatever this was. A not-nice item. Some sort of threat.

Pinch-punch was a kids' thing.

He turned the card around, wondering if looking at it upside down or sideways-on made the woods turn into a snarly face or the robin into a maggot crawling out of a bloody eye socket. Not that Mum would be bothered by macabre optical illusions. Her average Christmas Cruel was way worse. Her books were full of 18-rated violence and sex. Seven sensitivity readers told her to cut the thing on the last page of *Heidi Whose Husband Killed Her* but she left it in.

The house was cold. The radiators were fine – he knew where the bleed key was if there was a problem – and the lights sparkled or glowed as per Mum's diagram. It was another kind of coldness. Rust went along with much of Wickings Christmas for Mum's benefit. It felt strange in this limbo – waiting for her to get back to her proper personality and finish checking off her list. He couldn't remember all the traditions. Especially not the ones he was sure she made up fresh every year.

Left to his own devices, he did schoolwork. Next September,

41

he'd go to Sedgwater College. For now, he was partially home-schooled, partially online and at Ordinary School for exams and summer activities. It was Mum's idea to pick and mix his education. She had a teaching qualification like Nana and Grandad, but only ever used it on him.

He had worried other kids would think he was a mad behavioural science experiment – then found other kids were pretty much all weirdos. Mum called Ordinary School 'Shawshank' after a prison in a film she liked. Rust hadn't started his sentence by picking a fight with the biggest, most tattooed kid in class. Instead, he was signed up for multiple clubs by Perry and Skye Peason.

Being home in December was supposed to give him time to enter fully into the spirit of Christmas. Now he worried he was trapped at Six Elms for the duration by something more insidious than a flood.

He texted the Peasons an enigmatic 'hah huh?' in the hope of getting an explanation for the card – but just got spook emojis from Skye.

When Mum didn't come into the sitting room in the evening for the first episode of a Swedish TV serial about ritual child murder she'd highlighted in the *Radio Times*, he was up in the air. He didn't want to begin a serial without her. They liked shouting 'cheer up' and 'turn a bloody light on' at alcoholic inspectors poking about in dark cellars for frozen corpses. He synced his tablet to the system and cast YouTube haunting clips to the screen. The more they blew up, the faker they looked. 'It's not what you see or hear that's frightening,' said an American who'd bought the home where a 1990s pop star hanged himself, 'it's what you *feel*.' Rust gave up on finding pod material and endured half an episode of *Botz Boyz* without even getting angry. He turned to the mantel for comfort, but the Gargantuabots cadre were under the stairs. There was only that bloody card. Had the red breast splotch dribbled? No, he was being a nutter. It was probably inherited.

He turned off all devices – except the Christmas lights – and went to bed.

He lay awake, aware Mum was still up. He shut his eyes… then opened them to cold light, realising he'd forgotten to draw his bedroom curtains.

His bedside clock showed 08.57. He must have been awake for hours, then fallen deep asleep.

He went downstairs. Mum was up. Her first-thing mug was on the drainer by the sink. The kettle was still warmish.

She was back in her office. The door was shut.

He presumed she'd been to bed and slept.

He made himself tea and thought about a lidless mince pie for breakfast. He could still taste yesterday's foul chocolate. He had a tummy twinge – maybe anxiety, maybe the calendar seed sprouting in his gut. He drank tea from his Gretelgeuse toby jug.

He took up his tablet. More texts from the Peasons – none alluding to card-related strangeness. The twins wanted him to come to their cool school carol concert. They'd copied a Wickings idea and written new words to old tunes, but theirs weren't funny or cruel just different and massively smug. Someone had left a comment in Chinese on his pod board and it was a fiddle to copy the symbols into a translation tool. The results came back spam. Someone in Taiwan trying to sell him a barbeque set. The standard of feedback was usually higher.

Knocking on the office door was out of the question.

He played an online strategy game with an algorithm one level up from his current ability status and got hammered. He tried to build a wall but bricks kept evaporating when he put too much strain on them.

He often wished Mum would leave him alone for hours.

Guess what? This Christmas that dream had come true. And he was worried about it.

He looked at the bloody card again.

Still just a card. Wood. Robin. Snow. Star.

Merry Christmas. Pinch-punch…

'…and no return of any kind,' he said out loud.

He ran a system check on the decorations. All working perfectly. He went into the yard to make sure the exterior set-up had survived early morning frost. It was nippy out. Scarf, hat and gloves weather. He came back in quickly.

Mum's office door was still closed. With a gold-sprayed wreath on it.

It was quiet out as well as cold. They only got weather noises this side of Sutton Mallet. No passers-by. Few dogs. Not even much birdsong – the ghost of whatever Fillip had been kept the chirrupers away. Or else the crouching stones did a great job of warding off all comers.

A sound cut through the quiet. 'Pa-rum-pa-pum-pum.'

The Milk Float was coming.

The office door opened and Mum shot out. She wore ochre leggings and a knitted dressing gown/housecoat that came down to her knees. She moved past him at a clip…

'Skates on, slowcoach,' she said.

…and hauled the front door open.

The orange lights were going back down the Cut-Off.

'Drat, I wanted to talk to Petal,' said Mum.

'She's off,' Rust told her. 'I saw a replacement yesterday.'

Mum didn't hear him. She hopped across muddy concrete to the mailbox. The flag was up. Post was delivered. Mum was barefoot. She often slipped off her slippers while writing but usually remembered to slip them on again when she stopped.

He thought of stroking a stone for luck.

Mum sorted through the post. The soles of her feet must be freezing. She dropped items in see-through plastic or with illustrated envelopes – a wine catalogue, a magazine for sexy suspense writers that was all complaints about publishers. Next week's recycling, when someone – and he knew who that would be – troubled to pick it up and put it in the receptacle. Mum kept other pieces of mail. Cards.

Coming into the house, she brandished an envelope at him.

Here was that overly elaborate font again. Letters with too many curlicues – not written with pen or coughed out by printer but applied by a needle-pointed cake-icing gun loaded with squid ink.

To Master Russell Wickings,
Six Elms House,
nr Sutton Mallet, Somerset.

Mum pointed to the number beside the stamp. '2'.

There were other cards. Mum wasn't interested in them. Without opening, she knew they were from their dental practice in Hallam, a very old crime writer who was envious of Mum's sales (which showed how much he knew) and also fancied her, and a coupon from Charlie Chen's (the Takeaway Place That Delivers).

She steered Rust into the sitting room and sat him down at

the desk. They were doing over yesterday's ritual the way the police recreated the daily routine of a murder victim to jog witnesses' memories.

Mum gave him the card and his scalpel. Then looked him in the face, expecting him to take his cue.

'Aren't you going to open your window?' he asked. 'It's your turn for horrible chocolate.'

She paused… then opened the second window on the advent calendar and took out the sweet, which she didn't eat but put on the windowsill.

'What's the picture?' he asked, putting off the moment…

'Two red smudges, like evil Santa eyes,' she said.

She showed him. The smudges glared.

She tapped the envelope in his hand.

'Yes,' he said. 'Evil Card Alert. Still mental, I see.'

She tapped again, more insistently.

'Mum, it's a joke. You said so. Let's not be mugs.'

She took the envelope away.

'I'll open it then,' she said.

'It's addressed to me.'

'But it's aimed at me.'

She slid her forefinger into the envelope and ripped it open. The tear was jagged, like paper teeth. She should have used the scalpel. She took out the card.

It was the same picture.

Woodland at night. Robin redbreast with scarf. Deep and crisp and flipping freezing.

He took the card and examined it. Maybe the robin's beak was a smidge more open. Hitting a higher note in its warble.

'"Burble burble *second*, burble burble *beckoned*",' Mum said.

He opened the card.

Wait a second, something beckoned

Was the robin reacting to a beckoning? Eyes shifting to something off the edge of the frame.

Mum slumped, numb. How scared was she? Should he be scared too?

'…it's not a thing, no, not a real thing, not… no. Just no.'

He touched the robin on the front of the card. Red came off on his finger.

'Ink's still wet,' he said. 'That's shoddy.'

It wasn't the colour of blood but of red ink.

Mum coughed up a little squeak – a stifled scream.

'All right, Mum. I give up. I don't get it. What's this about?'

She breathed deliberately, calming herself down.

'*A Christmas Ghost Story*,' she said. 'I told people once – then I stopped because no one listened. I accepted it as a blip of my imagination. You know how you say my imagination is my super-strength and my own worst enemy. Well, it got away from me that time. "The Cards" was a story I made up the way I make up stories. But this is… is not a blip, not an echo. It's *targeted*.'

'Mum, have you gone mental? *More* mental?'

She got up and put the card on the mantelpiece, next to the first one.

```
Three cards on a shelf in Wychward Cottage.
The throat-cut robin has more blood in each
new picture. Its eyes are angry yellow. Its
little beak grows sharp teeth. The blood-
watered shoot becomes a shrub, already taking
the arrow-point shape of a fir tree.
```

Rooke strokes the top edge of the latest card
in place and cuts his finger open. He sucks
his own blood.

Nasty little sprig. A Holly Child. Unforeseen.
But of no moment. I am much changed, so
you're no worry to me. Though our postbag
becomes monotonous.

∽

More cards came. Bad news every day.

The same address in curly olde-timey writing. A number by the stamp as if Rust were likely to forget the date. A fresh message daily. The same woodland scene, only with spot-the-difference changes.

With the cards lined up on the mantel – they'd have to bunch up if a full set of twenty-four were delivered – Rust could sit on the sofa and swivel to see the picture in jerky motion. Like an animation. Or a stain soaking through cloth.

The robin was shrieking...

Behind the trees, a shape formed... white and blobby, with twiggy limbs. A lumpy head gave the impression of a face, eyes closed, mouth shut.

It wasn't yet in focus. Or near enough to see what it was. A snowman, perhaps?

The advent calendar was in the bin, dropped from the ritual. The soft centre Mum took out on the second day disappeared before he could put it in an evidence packet for chemical analysis. Whenever he remembered the sweet he ate, Rust felt a bit sick – as if that not-chocolate were still inside him, making mischief.

The messages were odd little stings...

DECEMBER THIRD, HAVE YOU HEARD...?

DAY THE FOURTH, WIND FROM THE NORTH.

MADE IT TO FIVE, ALL STILL ALIVE?

Mum got more mental. For a mid-week stretch, she became obsessed with catching whoever was driving the Milk Float, to intercept the cards at point of delivery, if not source. Something always distracted her or got in the way. Once, the front door stuck and wouldn't open until the 'rum-pa-pum-pum' van was receding. The door had stuck before. It was the cold. Probably. There was frost on the ground in the mornings now, thicker and longer lasting every day.

Another time, she was consumed with an urge to hunt down a stray lightbulb in the Christmas display. It flickered on and off when the house was looked at from the far field, though the string seemed unbroken if examined close up. Mum was in the far field, counting along roof-tiles to identify the treacherous light, when the 'pa-rum-pa-pum-pum' sounded. Another missed opportunity.

She planned an elaborate deception – making footprints in the frost to suggest she was gone for a walk further than the far field rather than hiding in wait in the lean-to while Rust reluctantly took up position halfway down the Cut-Off to prevent a getaway. The plan fell apart when the tarpaulin came off the woodpile. The flapping leathery gargantuakite had to be chased on the forecourt before it was gone forever. Mum was all for letting it fly free but if rain soaked the wood, it'd never burn and they'd have to rely on the radiators. Rust was sure Petal's replacement stood by the mailbox while they chased the tarp as if performing some country folk ritual like cheese-rolling or Morris-dancing. He still couldn't describe the post-person, except to be sure they were too pale to be Jamaican.

As they wrestled the tarp back over the pile, Mum noticed a fresh pea-green plant among the logs. It grew on cut wood like a mutant amalgam of mistletoe and seaweed. At nodes, it sprouted translucent ravioli packets. When popped like bubble-wrap, these turned out to contain hard little black pips. What on earth had a winter freeze growth spurt? Nothing – it must be an alien incursion. Mum had Rust hammer the tent pegs which secured the tarp's guy-ropes deeper in the frozen dirt. Starving the invasive weed of sunlight ought to do for it.

Rust flicked the nasty, sticky pips off his fingers.

WEDNESDAY SIXTH, A CAT-TONGUE LICKS...

DECEMBER SEVEN, FAR FROM HEAVEN...

NUMBER EIGHT, THE HAND OF FATE.

They kept up a grim procedure every morning. They'd open the day's card, read the off-kilter rhyme, peer at the picture, then place the offending item on the mantel with the others. Ordinary cards got ignored. E-cards were deleted.

This must be what people meant by 'beyond a joke'. It started weird then never got funny. Which was why he still suspected the Peasons, who were too busy with their concert to get back to him and explain themselves. In a follow-up Skype, the poltergeist-plagued vicar said he didn't know anything about the cards. He was embarrassed he'd *not* sent Rust a

Christmas card, though Rust didn't plan to send him one. He also said the knocking had died down.

Rust carefully re-read everything posted about the Paraphenomenon Pod since he started, trying to spot a malicious wrong 'un. Even the abusive or time-wasting comments – a *lot* were from a user in New South Wales – didn't read like the work of whoever made up the card messages. The unknown seasonal greeter could spell and wasn't addicted to RANDOM CAPITALISED WORDS in rants that went ON AND ON AND ON so you had to scroll down the page to get to the end.

Some messages were pithier or more pointed than others – the 'cat-tongue licks' one was properly naff. A few read like Christmas Cruels, which gave him a chill. A thought he did not want to have kept fluttering in his back-brain, like a moth against a window.

On the 'hand of fate' day, Mum admitted she'd had the same thought.

She said she wasn't sending the cards herself. Too obvious.

She told him about a film, *Who is Harry Kellerman and Why is He Saying These Terrible Things About Me?* He later watched bits of it on YouTube. A songwriter had trouble because someone called Harry Kellerman sent poison pen letters about him to his friends and associates. The songwriter couldn't find out who Harry Kellerman was and his life and career fell apart… only for it to be revealed (big surprise) he was writing the letters himself and signing them Harry Kellerman. Whether he knew what he was doing or had plot device amnesia wasn't clear.

Mum said she was not Harry Kellerman – or Tyler Durden, Mr Hyde or Norma Bates.

Of course, she *would* say that. In *Honey Homicide*, it turned out there never had been an apiarist ex-husband and Honey herself was training killer bees to sting her friends to death. The narrator had a split personality. Most readers guessed. One annoyed book-buyer posted a one-star review on Amazon that gave away the ending and ran to paragraphs about how bees can't be trained to commit murder. Was 'Kindle User Buzz' a suspect worth pursuing? Rust couldn't see a connection between a ticked-off bee-keeping mystery fan and a slow-motion flick-book of a scary Christmas scene.

He had to convince Mum he *didn't* think she was Harry Kellerman.

'I know it's not you,' he told her. 'Even you wouldn't do "the calls are coming from inside the house". Not after the bee book.'

'Thank you very much, I don't think,' she said.

'If you *were* sending them—'

'I'm not.'

'I know, but if you were…'

'…in an amnesiac fugue or second personality?'

'Yes, that. If you were doing this, you'd have to post a card every day.'

She blinked at the obviousness of the statement, then saw what he meant. She seized on his thought so eagerly he knew she'd worried she was responsible for the cards.

'I've not been near a pillar box all week,' she said, relieved. 'I've been here. With you. A witness.'

'You could have sneaked out when I was asleep,' he said, which made her face fall a bit. 'What I mean, Mum, is that it wouldn't work. Not with Christmas post. You'd have to gamble on next day delivery. Including Sundays when I'm not sure even Petal would warm up the Milk Float. After a week, the odds would be ridiculously long. One or more cards would be delayed, or arrive two at a time, or out of order. A card a day regular as an advent calendar isn't believable. The Royal Mail isn't like that.'

Mum was astonished.

'*That's* what you don't believe?' she said. 'You can accept flying saucers and EVP and poltergoonies and crop circles and all manner of oogedy-boogedy foofaraw... but not a regular postal service? Goat in Hilversum, what hath this century wrought?'

They both laughed, though neither saw much of a funny side. When Rust laughed, he felt jagged glass in his tummy.

Mum kept the envelopes the cards came in. They were post-marked from places in Somerset – Sedgwater, Hallam, Yeovil. They'd been posted in boxes, gone through a sorting office, and got bundled with the rest of the Six Elms mail.

NINE OF TWELVE, LINED ON A SHELVE...

COUNT TO TEN, THEN DO SO AGAIN...

ELEVENTH HOUR, FALL FROM A TOWER.

Fed up with the game, Rust swept the mantel and took the cards to the recycling. Mum was relieved for about ten minutes and manic with it. Then, she had a panicky turn and insisted on retrieving the full set and putting them back. He spotted she had them in the wrong order and rearranged them.

That white twiggy thing might even change every time he looked at the cards. It was an optical illusion, not something evil playing hide and seek. What was it? A snowman or a pudding, with barbed leaves and poison berries? A scarecrow wood skeleton clad in earth and snow and ice, hiding knife-sharp ribs in its mulchy softness?

It was increasingly difficult to get Mum to talk – or think – about anything else.

But she still wasn't telling him something. She was like this when working on a book. She wouldn't say what it was about or even what it was called until she had the end in her mind.

Rust did schoolwork but his remote assessors were already in end of term mode. Mum said teachers had carol concerts to worry about. The Peasons posted rehearsal clips from theirs, which the Head saw and didn't approve of – so the concert was called off. Local news took an interest ('Porn Panto Gets Axe'). The controversy generated a heated comment string. Perry and Skye were more pleased to be cancelled than they would have been if the show had gone ahead.

He played online strategy games. His ranking took a beating since he was getting worse and worse. He blamed cold fingers – it was close to freezing outside and hard to warm any room in the house – but knew his concentration was off. What Mum called his dicky tummy didn't help. That calendar choc was still staying where it was. He knew he hadn't passed it.

The weed in the woodpile didn't die, but spread thick tendrils out from under the tarp. It grew up around the window frame, winding around lights and decorations. Rust couldn't identify the plant online, but it wasn't exactly his field of interest or expertise.

The cards kept coming.

TWELFTH TODAY, RUN FAR AWAY . . .

THIRTEEN UNLUCKY... CHEERS ME DUCKIE!

FOURTEENTH E'EN, REMAINS TO BE SEEN.

He told Mum the rhymes were getting worse.

'I know,' she said.

'Not worse as in scary,' he said. 'Worse as in pathetic.'

'Well, I'm scared.'

'Don't be,' he said, irritated, and left the room to find something else to do.

He read ghost stories. As a paraphenomenologist, he disapproved of made-up ghost stories. They distracted from authentic cases. But he had to do homework about fictional ghosts. Too many chancers claimed experiences which turned out to be copied from books or films. Those *Insidious Conjuring Activity* films had a lot to answer for.

Mum never threw a book away. In the attic she kept Nana's 'aga sagas' (a term Mum had to explain which Rust promptly didn't understand again) and Grandad's manuals for outboard motors and model aeroplanes. A small back room was lined with floor-to-ceiling bookshelves. Under rows and rows of thrillers, whodunits, classics and biographies was a spook section. Collections of stories by M. R. James and Algernon Blackwood, thick old hardcovers with titles like *A Century of Creepy Stories* and an incomplete set of a paperback series called *The Fontana Book of Great Ghost Stories*. Mum was missing the sixth and eighth books; Rust had ordered copies off AbeBooks and was giving them to her for Christmas – filling gaps that had always offended him somehow.

What annoyed Rust about made-up ghost stories was that they tried to be frightening. To a researcher, paraphenomena

weren't frightening. The paranormal was like the weather –
you coped with it, enjoyed it if it was nice, didn't grumble if
tiles blew off your roof, and took care not to wander into a
thunderstorm waving a lightning rod. He didn't believe ghosts
were even ghosts in the way most people meant ghosts – the
spirits of the unquiet dead – but disruptions of the physical
world by as-yet-uncategorised energies which might or might
not have intent or consciousness. Taking these disruptions as
ghosts or aliens or angels or the Swine of Sedgemoor was
like seeing faces in clouds or woodgrain. Pretty, sometimes
– but not helpful. Made-up stories had characters, twists,
explanations; real hauntings seldom did. In made-up stories,
ghosts were out to get people. For revenge or from sheer
cruelty. A diet of books and films fostered shabby thinking
– many witnesses had so much spookery in their heads that
their testimony was too tainted to be useful.

Presuming a paraphenomenon was out to get you personally
– the curse theory – was presumptuous. A way of pretending
the whole world revolved around you.

Mum, he suspected, subscribed to the curse theory.

FIFTEENTH DAWN, WEEP AND MOURN...

Angie put the card on the mantel.

The Holly Child was taking shape – and getting nearer.
More trees were behind it than in front now.

Russell sat by her desk, bored and scared. Not a great
combination. Bored, scared and in the dark.

She thought she was protecting him.

All those grown-ups who said stories couldn't hurt you were wrong.

Six Elms House was literally being haunted by a Ghost Story.

For a week or more, she'd been close to spilling the beans. She held back because she didn't want to put a story – a meme – in her son's head which would make things worse. But living with her under this siege was not good for him. Whatever her mum and dad said or did to confuse or embarrass her, she never thought they were dangerous. A few more days of her being mental – kids still said 'mental', though it sounded outmoded and offensive even in phrases like 'mental health issues' – and Russell would be more afraid of her than of the cards. She bet he hadn't given up on the Harry Kellerman explanation. To him, it must make sense. She didn't tell him how she knew he wasn't a Harry Kellerman himself – because that wasn't the twist of 'The Cards'.

Russell was afraid of the cards, no matter how scientific he tried to be.

And he was right to be scared.

But wrong to be afraid of her. As she was wrong not to tell him the story – not the whole story, because she didn't have it. Could she even entirely trust her memory of what she did know? She wasn't going to sit him down like those lads M. R. James terrified with shit-scary tales in a candlelit study in Christmases gone by. She would meet Rust Wickings, Paraphenomenologist, on his own terms and offer her case history.

Maybe there'd be helpful answers in the comments – *hah!*

'Get out your podcatting kit,' she told him. 'I've a subject for you. Close to home. A paraphenomenon.'

∽

Rust saw through it. This was a Mum wind-up. A massively over-elaborate one.

She was thinking of a story and putting them both smack in it.

She was really scared. But she was scaring herself.

He had to let her go on. When she sprang her 'gotcha', he had to be ready with his 'gertcha'. That was the wind-up game.

He was offended she wanted to pull his podcast into it. She usually made a show of taking it seriously. Her parents treated her first writing as just more of her making up stories. Lying, they meant. They skimmed pages and said 'very nice, dear' but reckoned she'd grow out of it and teach Geography and get married. Without meaning to, Nana and Grandad were masters of what Mum now diagnosed as microaggressions. She quit writing for the best part of twenty years, though she avoided the chalkface and a wedding dress. She promised she wouldn't micro or macroaggress Rust out of his own bliss – though she deliberately said 'podcats' when she knew better. He didn't rate the Angie Wickings origin story. It's not as if anyone blew up her home planet when she was little.

He pinned the mike to her housecoat and checked the room for background hum.

'Say something Christmassy,' he told her.

'"Something Christmassy",' she said, like a five-year-old.

Red lines bounced on his tablet.

'More,' he said.

'... and the Angel of the Lord appeared unto the shepherds of Bethlehem and said, "Get the flock out of here – this is cattle country!"'

The red lines evened out.

'Fine.'

They set up in the sitting room. Mum was in an armchair by the fireplace, the row of cards on the mantel behind her. She gripped a mug of green tea with both hands for warmth. They'd not set a fire yet and the radiator needed help. The Christmas lights stayed on but he muted the winter wonderland soundscape. He doubted this session would make a droppable pod but couldn't abide tech sloppiness. Even dummy run-throughs should meet the quality threshold.

Until now, Mum had spurned all hints she appear on his pod. She said she was just a phenomenon and not remotely paranoid. She knew para was for -normal not -noid and was – despite her vow – being microaggressive with the deliberate mistake. She was trapped in an eternal cycle of doing unto Rust what had been done unto her.

Today, she *insisted* he record her.

He usually had days to do prep. He followed the trial lawyers code of never asking a question he didn't already know the answer to. The parabenighted needed prompts to tell their stories simply and directly.

Mum scratched the mike as if it were a burr on her dress.

'Please don't,' he said. 'Followers take the scraping for EVP – electronic voice phenomena.'

'And that's bad? Don't they follow you for phenomena?'

He ignored the microdig and ploughed on.

'I'll tell you what I tell everyone who comes on the pod. Don't worry if what you say doesn't make sense. Paraphenomena often don't. Or they'd be regularphenomena. Don't worry about droning on…'

'Thank you very much…'

'I'll edit for fluffs and repetition.'

'I've been interviewed before, Russ— Rusttt.'

This was spiky. Mum wasn't relaxing.

He had his prelim on his tablet but didn't need to look down. Garglebaskets Go Go Go, as Mum used to say – an earlier version of winding him up.

'Welcome, friends and followers, to a seasonal edition of the Paraphenomenon Pod,' he said. 'This is Rust Wickings, coming to you from the most haunted village in England. Remember: click like and subscribe. If enlightened, post on the comment board or send a message…'

'Unless you're a troll, perv or stalker, then leave my son well enough alone.'

'Friends and followers, meet my mother, Angelica Wickings…'

'…Queen of…'

'…(Self-Published)…'

'…Suspense.'

'Author of such books as… what are they again, Mum?'

'*Mistress Murder, Samantha Stalked*…'

'*Reggie Robbery, Algernon Assault, Fred Fraud*…'

'Cheek. Though *Fred Fraud*'s good. I'm having that.'

'So, established – my mother concocts *mysteries* for a living.'

'*Almost* a living. All titles available through your online vendor of choice… Click like and subscribe and buy…'

'Don't do ads, Mum. I'll get spam-blocked.'

She angled her head towards the lapel-mike. 'All I'm asking, Rust's followers, is that you send money. Email us your parents' credit card details. Remember to include the three little numbers on the back to qualify for access to the dark web – where all the mondo spook stuff lives. Much spookier than this.'

'No need to lay it on thick.'

'Trying to keep it light so I don't scream, okay?'

'So noted.'

They both took a breath.

'Christmas cards,' he read from his tablet. 'Snow, Santa, robins, stars, trees, kings, donkeys, shepherds. Season's greetings. An outmoded tradition. Snail-mailed, arriving in January. Signatures you can't make out. Profits for the Royal Mail. Or – terrifying messages from beyond time and space? Listen to my mother…'

'Words you rarely hear… "listen to my mother".'

She took a deep breath.

'When I was little, I wanted people to listen,' she said. 'Some did, but they were no help. I told a story. Not one I made up, though everyone said I did. I convinced myself I *had* made it up. A thing couldn't have happened, so I decided it hadn't. I tried to figure out how it got into my head, then gave up. I thought it was done with. One of those things you survive then try not to think about so you can get on with your life. Then, this year, on December the First, my son opened a card, the first card…'

'I'd just eaten a poison pellet from a sketchy advent calendar. We've noted this before. Omens and intimations, little strangenesses which presage major paraphenomena.'

'If you've any idea what that means, answers on a postcard, please.'

'Mum… Angie,' he said, 'tell us a story.'

She inhaled fumes from her mug but didn't drink.

'I'd say it was ancient history, but I know you're interested in ancient history, Rust. You have firm ideas of Angles and Vikings and flint-axes and standing stones. This is less-ancient ancient history, the blurry bit between Magna Carta and you being born. You know, when dinosaurs ruled the levels.

61

Chocolate came off the ration. We landed on the moon. One of those was before *I* was born. Both were a big deal to Nana and Grandad, who told me about them when I was little. They kept telling me about them till well after I was your age. You know a film comes over your eyes when anyone says, "When I was your age"? You've inherited it from me. I got fed up with grown-ups saying it too. I was younger than your age when "The Cards" happened. There, you've perked up. Yes, this is about "The Cards". All will now be revealed, as far as possible.'

He could scalpel a decent sentence out of that, he thought.

'This is Six Elms House,' she said. 'On its own on the Somerset Levels, near a tiny place called Sutton Mallet. I grew up here. I was a little girl in the 1970s and a teenager in the 1980s. I went to primary school in a big village called Hallam and the comprehensive in a small town called Sedgwater. Then college, then uni, then away… then back, when Dad was on his own. Then I decided to have you.'

'Less of the back cover copy,' he told her. 'Followers can look you up on Wikipedia.'

She spat. Wikipedia was a sore point. 'I'm sure it's Janet Speke making those edits to my page.'

'The cards, Mum. The Christmas cards.'

'Six Elms at Christmas,' she said. 'Except for two years in Germany with Mum and Horst, I've spent all my Christmases here. Christmas is a Wickings thing. We've always had the tree in that tub. We've always had mince pies with too much mince. We leave broken biscuits in Fillip's bowl to give the reindeer food poisoning so they skip High Ham. We wrap each other's presents in the paper they wrapped last year's presents to us in – or else pay a forfeit to the Tree Ghost. We sing Christmas Cruels – nasty or rude versions of Christmas songs. "We Wish

You a Hairy Christmas", "Santa Claus is Mugging a Clown". Well, we laughed. I know it's corny but Wickings Christmas was a joy, a reassurance, an acknowledgement that for a month or more the world generally turned to our satisfaction. Problems solved, God and sinners reconciled, presents under the tree, goodwill to all men and microbes. But there's another side to Wickings Christmas. A spooky side. I was quite afraid of the Tree Ghost, though I think my grandad made him up in stories he told your grandad when he was little…'

'You used to put the Tree Ghost in stories for me. I never minded.'

'And you turned out entirely uninterested in the super-natural.'

'Paraphenomenal. Fair point. You warped my mind and I should be taken into care. Meanwhile, back at the ranch…'

'Yes, Christmas. A big part of it in the 1970s was Christmas telly. Not just a Wickings thing, but an Everyone thing in the dim, dark, distant days. Janet Speke's friend Stacy Cotterill once asked to have her Christmas dinner on a tray so she could watch David Soul on *Top of the Pops*. When I was a child, before video recorders – remember video recorders? – before catch-up and iPlayer and streaming and YouTube and podcats and whatever comes next… there was just telly. An aerial on the roof, which needed fiddling with if a bird shat on it. Only three channels. Often three boring programmes at the same time. Then two films you wanted to see overlapping. You'd switch back and forth to follow both. That's how I saw *The Towering Inferno* and *The Railway Children*. Not optimal. You'd click a dial on the set to change channels. No remotes.'

'Yes, she's old,' Rust said into his own mike. 'Like and subscribe and buy her a stairlift.'

'An idea got into my head that the best telly went out after my bedtime. Much better than *Are You Being Served?* or *Crackerjack*. No matter how much I wanted to – and frankly I made a right pain of myself – Mum and Dad stuck firm to sending me up to my room at nine. No negotiation, no compromise. TV schedulers called nine o'clock the watershed, the point of the evening when children were presumed not to be watching. They showed Dennis Potter plays with nipples or Hammer horrors with fangs. I *heard* about after-bedtime telly. Other children had later bedtimes – or no bedtimes at all. At break, they'd tell about programmes they'd seen. In detail. It wasn't until later I realised other children were habitual little liars. Janet Speke hadn't seen *Emmanuelle Meets Frankenstein*. There isn't such a film. Actual after-bedtime telly in those days was the news in Welsh and Open University, but I didn't know that. To impressionable Angie, after-bedtime telly was the scariest of the scary. Scarier than the pig-man puppet in "The Talons of Weng-Chiang", which I still maintain was scarier than those gasmask brats in modern *Doctor Who*. After-bedtime telly was more frightening than masked rapists, hijackers and Maggie Thatcher Milk Snatcher. And the *scariest* after-bedtime telly of all was the Christmas Ghost Story…'

She paused for effect. Another podcaster might layer in chilling little bells.

'The BBC's Christmas Ghost Story was a tradition,' Mum continued. 'And you can find a list on Wikipedia if the entry hasn't been blitz-bombed by merry pranksters. It started on Christmas Eve, 1971, with an M. R. James story. "The Stalls at Barchester". It's out on DVD and I'm sure you can pirate it online. I've never seen it. For the best part of ten years, the BBC made a Ghost Story every Christmas. Janet Speke, all of two when "The Stalls of Barchester" was on, said she'd seen it. Janet Speke said she'd seen *all* the Christmas Ghost Stories. I said that was probably why her hair had gone white and she said she was just very blonde. Come to think of it, Janet looked like a ghost herself. We should have called her Janet Spook.'

'To the point, Mum, the point. Followers aren't here for your playground grudges.'

'How do you know? Anyway, Janet watched – or *said* she watched – all the late-night programmes and lived to tell the tale. She said *she* wasn't scared but that if *I* saw a Christmas Ghost Story I'd die. I was "of a nervous disposition" and the BBC warned people like me not to watch. It wasn't only Janet. Other kids joined in and described programmes they'd seen but I hadn't. Stacy Cotterill's bedtime was past midnight. I knew telly went off around midnight. Twenty-four-hour broadcasting didn't start in Britain till later. When I called Stacy a liar and showed her the shut-down time listed in the *Radio Times*, she said after midnight the BBC showed programmes too horrible to describe in the *Radio Times*. They'd be arrested if they owned up to making them. Imagine that. Also: imagine Little Angie believing Stacy.'

Was this the real reason Mum kept Rust away from Ordinary School? So he wouldn't mix with little liars?

No, that was ridiculous.

She ought to have got over this years ago – though maybe she hadn't and this was all about that. He only gave up a Harry Kellerman theory about Janet Speke when Nana mentioned off-hand some mischief Janet got Angie into on a march to support a miners' strike. Thanks to Janet, Mum had a criminal record for trespass and damage.

'Here's a funny thing,' Mum went on. 'On one hand, I

believed seeing the Christmas Ghost Story might kill me. Turn my hair white and stop my heart. On the other hand, I still ached to watch it. What I wanted was to be really scared then go on the playground and say I wasn't fussed. That'd shut Janet and Stacy up, right? Right.'

Mum paused, more sly than mental. She finally drank some tea. Then, on with the flashback...

'So, it's 1979,' she said, 'after my first term at Big School. I had to wear a blazer and tie and do homework. I decided I was grown-up enough to make my own viewing choices. I hunted through the double issue of the *Radio Times* for the Christmas Ghost Story. There it was... on BBC1, Christmas Eve. When did it go out? Eleven fifteen. After my bedtime. Even in school holidays, when I was allowed up till half past ten. I now know Mum and Dad worried when television frightened me. I had nightmares about Bagpuss. A puppet cat. It sat on my chest, poking my eyes with its stuffed tail. Still, I decided to go through official channels. I laid out my case. All my friends would watch the ghost story. So what was the harm? Mum told me I liked the *idea* of scary programmes but didn't like actual scary programmes. Dad supported me. He told Mum it'd be more frightening in my head if I *didn't* see it. He said they should watch the ghost story with me and explain how the special effects were done. He liked pointing out zips down the backs of monsters on *Doctor Who*. Which was more annoying than reassuring, if you want the truth – but he meant well. The verdict went against him. Mum and Dad planned to stay up late on Christmas Eve – soaking the pudding in spirits, mixing stuffing, cutting crosses into sprouts. They couldn't take a telly break from the cooking schedule. A ruling was made. I was to be in bed by ten thirty, stocking hung, lights out.'

She clicked her fingers, which would need to be muted.

'If I wanted a ghost story, I could read one from a book. Mum and Dad reckoned it was settled. They were already deep into the Christmas itinerary. I'd be out of bed before breakfast mince pie with too much mince to tear into the first presents. That was what it was about, my lover – pressies and stuffing. No telly until the Queen. She was only on with the sound off so Dad could sing his version of the National Anthem: "Cod Shave Our Stocious Queen". Wickings Christmas '79 was so big a production I doubt my ghost story was in the top twenty things Mum and Dad worried about. Gaffer and Poppette were coming for dinner. They were a whole other set of stickiness. They heard me singing "Adolph the Brown-Nosed Reindeer" and expected Dad to punish me. Decided frost around cracker-pulling time that year.'

Gaffer and Poppette – more ancient history. Nana's parents. Rust's great-grandparents, though Mum called them the not-so-great-grandparents. When Mum got arrested, Gaffer and Poppette broke off diplomatic relations for five years. The Iceni meant more to Rust, though he'd seen family photo albums.

'I went to bed. At ten o'clock. A full half-hour before curfew, to instil a false sense of security. I read a ghost story from a Fontana Book but it wasn't scary. Just weird. It was about a ghost combing its hair. Frightened? Me, neither. I turned out the lights. Did I go to sleep? I did not. I lay there, listening to clattering from the kitchen. I had not given up. I was determined – and stealthy. At five past eleven, I slipped out from under the blankets and put on my dressing gown. No slippers. They'd make too much noise. When I stepped on flagstones between rugs, I winced. Froze my toes. I think I still don't have full feeling back in my feet. I crept downstairs like a stealth ninja. Most of the year, the house was so dark I'd blunder into a coatrack or trip over a Dad contraption, but it was December. Wickings Christmas. Fairy lights strung in all the rooms and passages. Enough to see by. I knew every creaky board. We had them replaced later, when the rot set in. A big risk was passing the kitchen door, which lucky for me was shut to keep in the warm. A rim of light showed round the edges. I heard pop music, the Christmas charts…'

She sort of crouched in her seat, giving an impression of being small and shifty.

'I imagined my heart thumping,' she went on. 'If I was this scared just creeping out of bed, how bad could the Christmas Ghost Story really be? It wasn't that I *wanted* to be frightened rigid – much less die. I wanted to see for myself, to face the worst. And tell other kids. In 1979, what I wanted for Christmas was for Janet Speke to shut up and listen. Not a nice wish, but I'm not going to apologise for it.'

She pointed past the tree.

'I opened that door there,' she said. 'I nipped in and closed the door behind me. The click was like a rifle-report, but no one came running. I checked the room. Embers in the grate. Fillip's bowl by the chimney for Santa. A smell of teatime. Someone – *not* Jolly Old Saint Nick – had tipped broken biscuit bits into the fire. I appreciated the sacrifice element. Kids know all about making bargains with higher powers. It's why churches try to snatch 'em early.'

She looked at the enormoscreen.

'This was, oh, seven or eight tellies ago,' she said. 'When I was really little, we had black and white. This was our first colour set. You know when politicians complain about poor people being able to buy flatscreens and iPhones and avocados? Well, they used to say the same about colour TV.

A luxurious frippery. Dad held out, saying black-and-white films were the only things worth watching on the box – until David Attenborough's nature documentaries came on. That persuaded him to pay a higher licence fee and rent a new set. The screen was about a quarter of the size of that one, but the telly was in the same place. Not too near the fire. The black-and-white set used to take a minute to warm up, but colour TV came on in seconds. A BBC1 logo revolved: the world with Christmas icing on the top. I turned the sound down almost to nothing. I didn't want to attract attention. I was counting on tree lights to cover the glow around the door if Mum or Dad peeped into the hallway. I sat close so I could hear as well as see – yes, grown-ups warned me about googly eye syndrome. An announcer said...

'"The following programme is not suitable for those of a nervous disposition or children who should be in their beds..."

'The ghost story was called "The Cards",' Mum went on. 'It was set in 1850 or so. More Dickensian than M. R. Jamesy. The main character was Mr Rooke, a warlock who sacrificed the Spirit of Christmas to become a Joy Leech. A kind of vampire who sucked happiness out of people. It made him strong and them sick. He visited cheerful people and left hollow, unhappy shells. Leeching pumped him up. He got younger. He had powers. Flying, being invisible, probably x-ray eyes, I don't know. The *Superman* film came out around then and everyone had superpowers for a while. The Spirit of Christmas came out of something like the egg in *Alien*. This is important, by the way. There are things about "The Cards" I didn't understand as a kid which are obvious looking back – like special effects inspired by a film I didn't see for years.'

Rust reckoned seeing something forbidden by her parents compounded the effect – cubed the scariness. He'd sampled those old BBC ghost stories on YouTube and found them slow or slight. They hadn't had proper CGI in those days and had to use glove puppets and disco lights. Or sheets on fishing lines.

'Mr Rooke was bad,' Mum went on, 'though he was just an old actor with stuck-on sideboards. But the Joy Leech wasn't the worst thing. The warlock getting his wish was only the set-up. The story was about the murdered Spirit of Christmas getting revenge, coming back as something nasty. A Holly Child. Mr Rooke was tormented by Christmas cards, a different one each day, each more horrible than the last, each showing just a bit more of the Holly Child, pulling Rooke just a bit more into its bleak woodland limbo… where his horrid fate awaited. An extended "I'm going to get you". I know, I know… it's nothing compared with whatever you saw too young which scared you…'

She talked into her mike again, as if it were a third party.

'Rust begged and pleaded to be allowed to watch *The Walking Dead* when it started then didn't last five minutes, poor lamb…'

'Mum…'

'We're being truthful, right? What I mean is: scary is subjective. To me, to Little Angie, "The Cards" was the most terrifying programme I could imagine. You can see where this is going. I'll say that again for emphasis – maybe you could do a hollow echoey effect like those popular podcats – *"The Cards" was the most terrifying story I could imagine*… and it turned out I had. Imagined it.'

'There,' said Rust. 'That's it, that's the hook – like and subscribe and comment…'

'Can we get on with it now?' Mum asked.

'Aren't you supposed to be Queen of Suspense?'

'Princess of Wanting This Over With here.'

'This is your platform, Mu-Angie, please continue…'

'I should have listened to Mum and Dad,' said Mum. 'I was frightened rigid. I saw what I shouldn't have seen. I couldn't not think about it. I lay awake most of the night. Me being tired the next day was put down to getting up too early, like children always do. I was subdued that Christmas. I even said there might be *too much* too much mince in the mince pies with too much mince. Wickings Heresy. No, I didn't own up to breaking curfew. I thought the Tree Ghost would get my presents if I told. I understood the rule of silence. The Holly Child from "The Cards" was going to get me, I knew that… but if I blabbed to Mum and Dad, it would get me *worse*.'

'Pussilla.'

'Five minutes of *The Walking Dead*, Russell. And a wet bed. Bet you cut that.'

'Proceed…'

'I survived till New Year un-got. I didn't sleep well. I also didn't watch much telly. Mum and Dad must have noticed but they were busy with… well, Christmas. Gaffer and Poppette were a trial. Worse than the Brown-Nosed Reindeer time. Gaffer had voted for Mrs Milk Snatcher and went on about her night and day. Mum was in the NUT and CND and not a fan of the new Prime Minister. I kept schtumm. Until first break of first day back at Big School. When I'd get support, relief even. My friends would have the same war story. They'd all have seen "The Cards". If we shared how scary it was, it'd lose power. But I got blank looks. No one else saw the programme. Janet Speke – the biggest little liar on the playground – told me *I* was

lying, that I was mental in the head. Janet said there was
no such programme and I'd made it up. The other children
believed her, not me. Which was a good call. I *had* made
it up. Probably. I dug the holiday issue of the *Radio Times*
out of the bin – we didn't recycle then, because we were
determined to leave a dead planet to our unborn children.
I could have sworn there was a write-up for "The Cards".
A picture of Mr Rooke looking frightened with something
blurred and angry-eyed in the background. No, nothing.
That year, there *was* no Christmas Ghost Story. At the time
I was being terrified by "The Cards", BBC1 was showing a
Christmas Choir. A musical on the other side. More bloody
carols on the channel with adverts. So I dreamed it, right?
But I didn't dream it in bed. I really came down into the
telly room – this one – and huddled here, feet freezing, in
front of the box, eyes open... watching what? A horror
show projected on the inside of my eyelids.'

She looked over her shoulder, up at the mantelpiece. Cards
in a row.

'Now I want a refund on my brain. It's leaking into reality.'

```
A village sign - Rokesby Roylott. Bleak
December evening, enlivened by carol singers.
Sexton Fimple and his wife Margery, and three
village children - Betsey, Tristram and Pig
- are conducted by the Reverend Jepthah
Godly. They give forth 'God Rest Ye Merry
Gentlemen'. The choir shows more enthusiasm
than tunefulness. Their pastor's smile is set
like a crack...

...which invites a spectre to slip in among
them.
```

Rooke, spryer than before, wears a cowl and a long black cloak. The wassailers can't see him. He puts his hand against Godly's chest and pulls all joy out of him - stopping his baton-waving... then he darts into the choir and does the same, touching children's mouths and adult chests.

They fall silent.

Rooke is taller now, staggering as if drunk. He flaps away like an engorged bat.

The choir are shocked and don't know what's happened. Godly tries to sing again but can't find his voice. Margery sits in snow, face in her hands. Fimple weeps silently. Betsey scratches herself with mittens. Tristram is in a trance. Pig snuffles.

Up above, Rooke flies through clouds like a ragged blackbird.

God rot ye merry gentlebugs, let ae things ye dismay... heh heh ha ha... remember Hob your Pitchfork Lad was spawned on Christmas Day... Tristram rocks back and forth, traumatised... he repeats 'Dismay, dismay, dismay, dismay...'

So, 'The Cards' was off her chest. And on Russell's.

Interview concluded, Angie unpinned her lapel-mike. Russell stowed the recording equipment in its cases. She felt light-headed, almost tipsy. The jokester could come out from behind the curtains now and own up to a prank she was supposed to find hilarious.

If that was the explanation, she'd never sign the release form.

Russell went off to do 'research' – often a blanket term for online gaming or (she knew and he knew she knew) porn. He came down from his room three or four times that afternoon and evening. With follow-up questions prompted by actual research.

'Do you know what the Mandela Effect is?'

'The Mandala Effect?'

'No, Mandela. Like Nelson Mandela.'

'The South African leader? I know who he was.'

'You remember him dying in prison?'

'No. He didn't. He was in prison for a long time. But he came out, there were fair elections and the regime changed. I think he got a Nobel Prize and they made films about him. With Morgan Freeman. Then he died.'

'People remember him dying in prison.'

'They're wrong.'

'Yes, but even when they're told they're wrong, they *remember* it…'

She sort of saw what he was getting at, then he was back in his room.

Next time, he asked if she'd heard of *Shazaam*, a film about a genie with a comedian called Sinbad. She hadn't. The only genie film she could think of was the cartoon with Robin Williams.

'People online say they've seen *Shazaam*,' said Russell, 'but it's not real. There is a film about a genie called *Kazaam*, which is probably what they are thinking of.'

'With Robin Williams?'

'No, that's *Aladdin*. *Kazaam* starred a basketball player. But no one cares. It gets slated on Letterboxd and Rotten Tomatoes. What *is* interesting is people remember *Shazaam* in detail. Story, scenes, lines of dialogue, even a theme song. These people don't know each other... live in different countries... but swap memories of *Shazaam*. Memories they can't have. Sinbad says he's starting to believe he made the film, though he's just joking...'

'... being a comedian.'

'Yes. But, Mum, what happened to you has happened to others.'

Her heart skipped. Her mind wobbled.

'Other people saw "The Cards"?'

Russell looked down. 'Well, no... and it doesn't exist, so far as the internet can tell...'

'...which is infallible.'

'But other people have seen films and television programmes that don't exist.'

She wasn't comforted.

He said he'd do more research. She'd have been happier if he were on PornHub.

The next day, they went back to trying to catch the phantom postie. Mr Rum-Pa-Pum-Pum.

Rust and Angie, gloved and scarved against the cold, sat on the forecourt in garden chairs retrieved from winter storage in the lean-to. They staked out the mailbox, waiting for the Milk Float. The concrete was dusted with grit-speckled frost. Little icicles hung from the mailbox stand and the bars of the gate. Rust's ears were frozen. He should have worn his Gargantuabot Rex helmet. Mum had a Thermos of Baileys-laced coffee.

He hadn't completely digested the story of Mum and

'The Cards' and how it might be a manifestation of the paraphenomenon-adjacent Mandela/*Shazaam* Effect. Other podcasts had done episodes about shared false memories. He'd listen to them when he had time.

Today, he was looking at another part of the mystery.

Whoever was sending the cards knew about 'The Cards'. Enacting a story Mum was once a conduit for – or else made up because of premature onset bonkers in the nut syndrome. They should be grateful the unknown correspondent wasn't bringing *Honey Homicide* to life. Rust wasn't the first person Mum had told about her childhood strange turn. Knowing her, he suspected he was close to the last.

It still felt like a Peasons prank.

'Mum, weren't you at school with Perry and Skye's dad?' he asked.

'Pete Peason? Not school. He was at Sedgwater College when I was.'

'Did you tell him about "The Cards"?'

'No, college was years later. A lot happened between 1979 and 1987. I got a criminal record. Then I had A levels to worry about. I didn't know Pete well. He was a Young Farmer. I was a Young Anything Else.'

So he couldn't have passed the story on to Perry and Skye then. Drat. A dead end lead.

'It really isn't the twins, Russt.'

She was trying to call him 'Rust' not 'Russell' but the 's' always went on a micron too long.

'If it's not the Peasons, how about your arch-enemy? Janet Spook.'

Angie laughed, bitterly.

'Goat, she was a cow and a half. She got worse later. After

the arrest thing, her parents and mine agreed we should be barred from associating with each other. Probably a mercy for us both. Stacy Cotterill told me Janet started having visions and turned Crazy Christian. Joined a happy-clappy cult. More likely to send annoying leaflets than creepy cards.'

'What about this Stacy? A good suspect?'

'Stacy went another way. Ultra-girlie at college, then cut off her hair and joined the police. She's a DCI in London. I email her queries about procedure when I need to. She actually sends us a real Christmas card. It came a few days ago. Want to compare handwriting?'

Normally, Mum would have sent her own cards by now. In previous years, she'd presented Rust with a ream to sign. A robin or a snowman, proving she didn't have a long-lasting complex from 'The Cards'. He'd squiggle next to her practised signature. His next job was to pedal to Sutton Mallet and shove the Wickings cards in the pillar box. Wickings cards went by the wayside this year. DCI Cotterill wouldn't be getting a card back.

'You told other people at the time?' he said. 'Children.'

'No one listens to kids.'

'Tell me about it.'

'*Hah.*'

'Children grow up.'

'Mostly. But kids at my school weren't likely to grow up to be... well, sadistic warlocks.'

'Later on, at uni, in the years since...'

'*Many* years since.'

'Yes, many years since. You've told other people?'

Mum nodded. 'Jamie Marion was interested,' she admitted, 'though more in me than "The Cards". That was at uni. Jamie knew about the real Ghost Stories for Christmas. He was planning an oral history of spooky seventies telly. Probably inspired by me. I don't know how far he got.'

'Anyone else?'

'The last conversation I remember having about "The Cards" was with Daniel and I can't imagine him being behind this. The story hasn't come up often. Why would it? Folk you interview bang on about their ghost encounters or UFO sightings every other sentence. I'm more impressed with people you have to work on a bit to get to tell their story. The ones who are ashamed or embarrassed or haven't sorted out in their own heads what really happened.'

That was sharp. Mum had put into words something Rust had half-thought but shied away from. When his mother lost a chapter by crashing her computer or bought everything for her famous risotto recipe except the rice, it was easy to forget she was a bright spark. If prone to putting things together in counterintuitive, not always functional ways. Riceless risotto. *Warlock Wendy*. 'The Cards'.

'This is a thing that happened one time when I was eleven,' she went on. 'When you were eight, you broke your foot walking through the long grass on Sutton Mallet village green.'

Rust winced. He assumed there must be a hidden stone in the grass but there was nothing. He'd put his foot down wrong while wearing new Gargantuaboots and a toe-bone snapped. He had a black toenail for eighteen months afterwards. A medical puzzle, but a long way short of a paraphenomenon.

'How long do you go without mentioning the broken foot?' she asked. 'Is it regularly rehashed in podcats? Is your handle, Rustoncebrokeatoeongrass02? How often do you even think about it?'

'Whenever I get new trainers, you say "careful not to stub your toe".'

'Otherwise it's a dead issue, right. Done with and locked away. If it weren't for the cards, "The Cards" would be the same. A funny thing that happened one time. Not funny, odd. I would have told you about it eventually. We'd have been streaming a modern ghost story – *Amityville Henhouse* or something – and I'd remember. I'd have told you then. You wouldn't be impressed. Not a proper paraphen, is it?'

He'd had a think – and done some hunting.

'There are possibilities,' he told her. 'BSI.'

'Come again.'

'Broadcast Signal Intrusion. Audiovisual transmissions – random images and sounds – which take over regular channels for brief periods. Like the tape in *The Ring* but without the curse. It's happened several times. In America. And Russia. No one owns up to being behind it. No one knows where the signals come from…'

'Let me take a guess… nerds with too much time on their hands, too much tech in their mothers' basements, and a weird impulse to mystify.'

'Who does that sound like?'

'Besides you? Perry and Skye weren't born then. Can they broadcast signal intrude back in time?'

'It's a theory.'

'Sorry. I'm afraid I don't believe rival podcatters have invented time travel. Or could produce broadcast-quality spooky vintage television. I've listened to their show.'

'Traitor!'

'You go on about it so much, of course I listened. Yes, Pete Peason has bought them enough tech gear to found a media empire. But an overcompensating divorced dad can't buy the twins talent or imagination. It's genetic.'

She tapped his head and he cringed.

Sometimes, she showed she was proud of him.

'Yes, you're likely to go mental too,' she said. 'We can get matching mother-and-son straitjackets.'

'There might be a chronal displacement element.'

'You what?'

'Call "The Cards" a vision… a complex hallucination… whatever. It got to you somehow. Your eleven-year-old head was full of a ghost story you'd just read in bed and rumours about scary programmes from Janet and Stacy. Maybe this year's cards, wherever they come from, project an effect into the past, into your mind. A timeslip from now, from this situation, is translated into a form young you could understand. A TV show.'

'You mean "it was all a dream"? That's been the general consensus… until the cards started coming. They aren't a dream.'

'You make up stories for a living. You could have made this one up.'

'I wasn't that good at it then.'

'You're not that good at it now.'

She swatted him with a loose mitten. 'Which is why it's not much of a living.'

Rust had tabbed a few recorded BSI videos on paraphen sites. Most were people in masks looning about. Some included religious or political slogans. Typically, they were pointless. A clown in traffic with polka music. Migrating birds with the film run in reverse and poetry read backwards. Fractal patterns and drilling and hammering. Not stories – not ghosts.

The forecourt shook. An almighty *crack!* sounded.

Mum swore and dropped her Thermos. The noise came from round the back of the house.

What had the tarpaulin done now?

They ran to the scene. Yard-long ice spears had fallen from the gutter, taking a string of still-burning lights with them, and shattered on the covered woodpile. How had that made such a racket? Or shaken the ground? It had felt like a mortar attack.

'Goat, please not a white Christmas,' said Mum. 'Burst pipes, frozen firewood and no Charlie Chen's.'

'We got through flood year.'

'The pipes didn't burst… and the power stayed on. If we go Arctic, I guarantee the lights will fail. Like in the 1970s.'

'We'll live.'

'You'd live offline. No devices. No streaming. No uploads.'

'Point.'

Mum extracted the longest chunks of ice and threw them away. Dribbles from the gutter had frozen. Rust knelt down and did detail work, freeing the lights. It was a miracle half the wall hadn't come down with the iciclealanche.

'We'd better go round the eaves with a hammer to be sure there aren't any other danger zones where ice has built up.'

'You say "we", Mum…'

'You're much nippier than me, Rust. Agile, like Spider-Monkey…'

'…-Man. It's Spider-Man.'

'Couldn't it be Spider-Monkey? I bet they've done that. Spider monkeys are a thing. I've seen them pooing on David Attenborough.'

Mum sounded like she'd sniffed helium. She was laying it on thick again. It was her 'I'm frightened' tell.

Actually, it was Spider-Man's too. He always wittered on hysterically while dodging octopus arms or pumpkin bombs.

Rust was kneeling on a green mat. Tendrils of woven weed. The tarp was still tight over the woodpile, but points stuck up under it like stalagmites. The new plant's growth wasn't slowed by darkness.

Mum noticed the creeping vegetation.

'We should get in some paraquat,' she said. 'Or napalm.'

Gretelgeuse once gave Violet Kono – the girl mind-linked with Gargantuabot Mauve – a cute sunflower pot-plant as a gift to mark a truce. It grew to be a giant strangling monster threat and overran Gargantuabase Island. If Mum's imaginary ghost story were coming true, maybe the reality-warp brain-leak was also acting out 'Flower Power' (*Gargantuabots: The Series*, Season Three, Episode Twelve).

He felt around the growth, squelching the ravioli-sacs, and found a root tethering the weed to the earth. A scrap of red foil was around it, like a ring on a finger. He had to tear the foil to get it free.

'What's that?' Mum asked.

'You've seen it before,' he said.

On December the Second – which seemed longer ago than barely a fortnight – Mum had taken a wrapped chocolate out of the evil advent calendar and put it on the windowsill… then they got fixated on the second card, the 'something beckoned' one. Later, the choc had gone. With the window shut, it couldn't have rolled outside – but it had got out somehow, bounced on the woodpile, and fallen on non-stony ground. Then, it had sprouted through its wrapper.

'I said it was more like a seed than a sweet.'

If all this growth came from Mum's set-aside choc, what about the one he'd eaten?

Whenever he remembered that chocolate, he had psychosomatic pangs. When Mum mentioned his broken toe, he had a pang there too. If someone jogged his memory about the time he got stabbed in the back, he'd feel a sharp jab between his shoulder blades – which, in fact, he did just imagining it – though the back-stabbing never happened.

He didn't so much feel hurt as stuffed, as if the seed had swollen into a mass of sage, onion and breadcrumbs and filled spaces inside his body, clogging everything, slowing him down.

This was just him making himself ill. He was all right really.

'You don't look well, Russell,' commented Mum – exactly the wrong thing to say, since now he felt *awful*. She pressed the cold back of her hand to his forehead to see if he had a temperature. 'I hope you're not coming down with something.'

A 'pa-rum-pa-pum-pum' sounded. Every day, it was more mocking.

Mum was livid – at being distracted again, most likely.

They sped back to their abandoned chairs, but it was a lost cause.

The mailbox flag was up. The front of the little house couldn't close on today's bumper post. The run-up-to-holidays issue of the *Radio Times* had come, days after the double issue covering Christmas and the New Year. See, real mail didn't run to exact schedule. From Mum's agent came ARCs of books by writers who wanted to snatch the Queen of Suspense crown from her – but also wanted her to say she enjoyed their mysteries so they could put her name on their covers. Today's crop was *Stabbing Sally-Anne* and *The Girl Who*

Got Ground Up. Non-threatening cards had arrived – including one for Rust from that vicar. He should probably send him one back.

And here was the sixteenth 'The Cards' card, a razor blade in blancmange. Rust pulled it out.

He recognised the writing. He saw the number by the stamp.

Mum shook her fist at the Cut-Off. The Milk Float was gone.

'We should put down a strip with nails,' she said. 'Or dig a bear-pit.'

She took the card from him and turned it over, looking for clues.

'I'll open it,' she said.

'It's mine,' he said.

'I'm your mum. I'll take the bullet.'

She tore the envelope open, glanced at the card, then looked inside.

'What's the recipe today?' he asked.

TEN AND SIX, HOW'S TRICKS?

'Rubbish.'

She showed him. That was what it said.

'What does it even *mean*?'

She shrugged.

'Is the thing in the trees more distinct?'

'No,' she said.

He was almost relieved, then she went on…

'…but it isn't alone now. It has friends.'

She put the new card on the mantelpiece.

The twiggy snowman was quite substantial now and in front of the trees. Wreathed with holly and mistletoe, black coal eyes sunk deep in its head. The swollen robin perched on its shoulder like a pirate's parrot, slit in its breast leaking scarlet. She remembered a name from 'The Cards'. Robin Deadbreast. The twiggy snowman was the cocoon of the Holly Child. This was what you got when you tried to slay the Spirit of Christmas. It grew back, but angry.

In the starlit trees assembled stick figures with muskets and tall shakos. Wooden soldiers – like Dad's, but missing arms and eyes as if victims of rough play. Toy Soldiers back from a war of attrition, backpacks filled with spite against folk who'd cheered them off with a pa-rum-pa-pum-pum and fife. Behind them were other visitors – wonkier angels, wolves in shepherd-skins, scowling oranges on stubby legs.

A red veil floated across the sky.

The Holly Child was starting to smile.

Russell was more queasy than frightened. Had she neglected his meals? She hoped he wasn't snacking on expired yoghurts or un-defrosted pork pies while googling broadcast signal intrusions or Mandela Effects. She was usually attentive about his diet. Aside from that mystery broken toe, he was a healthy boy. She had no worries about him being taken into care. His skin looked greasy, but was dry to the touch. He'd started shaving this summer and had blood blots on his chin most days.

He was trying to think it through. His way of coping.

'Mum, how far are we into the story?'

'Sixteen of twenty-four – so, two-thirds in. It speeds up.'

He couldn't stop looking at the cards.

For her, it was all about today's picture and message. Earlier instalments didn't mean anything because today's picture supplanted them. They were discarded drafts. Russell was interested in the long sweep of the mantel, the process of change. He kept all the cards in mind.

'Let's go back over the story…'

'Oh Goat, no, Rust…'

'Think. What do you really remember about "The Cards"?'

'The whole thing.'

'No, you don't. Some days you remember the message… some days, you're surprised. With "eleventh hour, fall from a tower" you thought it was wrong. You saw something else when you were little, with "fall of a flower" in it…'

'Thinking about it, I got it wrong then. I was eleven, Rust.'

'But it's what makes me believe you really saw something. If you were making it all up now, you'd get it right. You said as much about people on my pod. How well do you remember the programme?'

Shuddering, she made herself concentrate. She looked at the patch of carpet where she'd piled cushions to make a viewing nest for herself. Goat, it was the same carpet and they even had some of the same cushions.

She pictured the opening images of 'The Cards'.

That washed-out, fuzzy look of pre-digital television. Reception was iffy out here on the levels. The best signal came from the wrong BBC, where half the programmes were in Welsh.

'I remember some scenes like I saw them yesterday,' she told him. 'Other bits are out of focus. I really shouldn't have been up so late. I probably nodded off. I used to do that – be keen on seeing a film shown late in the evening, then fall asleep. I still don't know how *The Postman Always Rings Twice* ends.'

'If it was all a dream, how could you fall *more* asleep and miss bits of it?'

'It's a blur. I remember the opening, with the Spirit of Christmas sacrificed by Mr Rooke – and the warlock sucking the joy out of carol singers and charitable gents and happy families, turning the village dance into chaos.'

'Sounds good.'

'You know the way we enjoy Scrooge hating Christmas but being bitterly funny about it more than we enjoy him being merry and bright and buying a turkey for the Cratchits? It was like that. Mr Rooke was horrible, but the story wanted the audience to enjoy him being mean to foolish, happy folk. To set him up for his comeuppance. While Mr Rooke was being horrible, the cards kept coming – the Spirit of Christmas reborn as the Holly Child, gathering its armies to swarm out and take revenge.'

'Holy Child?'

'No, Holly Child. A pun. Also, more pagan than Christian. Look at it.'

Russell did. It looked back. Hungry or angry? Both.

'How does the story end for the man getting the cards? Mr Rooke.'

'Not happily. He gets got. He gets got good.'

That didn't satisfy him. He was a nit-picker about plots. Dad had been too – so the spoilsport gene evidently skipped a generation.

'Why didn't Mr Rooke use his Joy Leech powers on the Holly Child?'

'Oh, Rust, I don't know. It was long ago and I only saw "The Cards" – or imagined I saw "The Cards" – once. Late at night, excited and afraid, possibly half-asleep. How well can anyone remember telly? What happens in… uh, the sixteenth episode of *Gargantuabots*?'

'"Lava Lumps", *Gargantuabots: The Series*, Season Two, Episode Three… Gretelgeuse makes a giant golem out of molten lava and it attacks Reykjavik.'

'Okay, bad example. You'll understand if you get old.'

'Do you remember any credits? Who wrote or directed? Who played Mr Rooke? Did anyone in it later become famous?'

'Nope. On all counts. I think it was based on a published story, but maybe I think that because other Christmas Ghost Stories were M. R. James or Dickens. The Mr Rooke actor was someone I'd seen in things – classic serials, sit-coms, police shows… He usually played government ministers, bank managers or tramps. He must have owned a lot of wigs and pairs of spectacles in different styles. He might have done an advert for gummy chews. Yummy Gummy Chews, maybe. I'm no good at names. There was a Harbottle in the opening titles, I think. "Based on the story by Harbotham Mitherswope" or somesuch. No use googling. I'm filling in syllables where I have mind gaps. Hargood Trimarine? If one of the dirty-faced village urchins was, I don't know, a young Daniel Craig, I wouldn't have clocked it. You only make those connections when you rewatch something later, after the bit actor has become a star.'

Russell tutted, impatient with his mum's fragmented memory.

'I'm sorry, Rust,' she said. 'I can only work with what I have.'

He sighed.

'It still convinces me you're not making it up. Like you

said… when someone is lying, the story makes sense and has a lot of detail. And it's the same every time they tell it. People trying to be truthful aren't sure and have blanks or don't agree with themselves from session to session.'

Now she wanted to hug him, but was concerned he might actually sick up. He'd been going around looking like he was about to for days.

'What was it like the years after?'

'You mean, were there repeats of "The Cards"? No. It didn't turn up on a video and haunt me again. Mr Rooke hasn't crawled out of my monitor. No signal intrusions until this year. I gave myself a phobia, though. For a while, with Mum and Horst, I was well off Christmas. And Christmas is *enormous* in Germany. *Grosse Weihnachten*. When I came back to Six Elms I had to get over that. For Dad. He *needed* Wickings Christmas. Especially after the divorce. Continuity, I suppose. We worked hard to go back to basics. Mince pies with too much mince. Christmas Cruels. Wrapping presents in last year's paper. We kept it up, even when I was home from uni… even after Dad died, I kept it up, for me as much as for you. I wanted you to have Wickings Christmas, Rust. Not a nightmare every December. Wickings Christmas had been spoiled for me – by my own fault – and I determined to unspoil it for you. And I did a bloody good job, if I do say so myself. That phobia, though… it was tough to get past.'

'What were you phobic *of*?'

'What else. Being got. By the Holly Child. I was terrified it would get me.'

Russell held his chin, an I'm-thinking-like-a-detective gesture he'd started using before he could walk and hadn't yet grown self-conscious about. She tried hard not to use it back at him, for fear she'd freeze it out of his repertoire. Some part of Rust had to remain adorable or she'd failed as a mother.

'This Mr Rooke in "The Cards" was a villain,' Rust said. 'He murdered a baby.'

'A made-up villain and a weird spirit baby. It had a beard.'

'But Mr Rooke deserved it. He deserved to be got. He was guilty. It's not scary in a story when a bad thing happens to a bad person. It's justice.'

Now, she did hug him – only lightly and briefly.

'Oh, poor love, that's not how scary works. To you, it's all puzzles – paraphenomena. Mysteries with answers. A bad person getting got is scary because everyone thinks they're bad, that they deserve to be got. I'd snuck down to watch "The Cards" despite being told not to. Not murder, but a crime. A trespass. I felt guilty about it. A smidgen of shame was enough to provoke the wrath of higher powers. And lower ones.'

'You can't still be scared that the Holly Child will get you.'

'No. Of course not. That'd be ridiculous. I'm a grown-up. The cards aren't addressed to me. I'm scared the Holly Child will get *you*.'

Rust thought he'd had a breakthrough.

In his bedroom late at night, he found an online *Radio Times* archive. Wikipedia said the Ghost Story *for* Christmas series ended in 1978. But the BBC still broadcast a ghost story *at* Christmas in 1979. Disguised as an art documentary, 'Schalcken the Painter' – 'a chilling tale of the supernatural' – went out more or less in the slot where Mum put 'The Cards' but a day earlier. She *could* have got the date wrong. Maybe

Nana and Grandad went out on Christmas Eve and did their pre-dinner prep on the 23rd. Sprouts with crosses cut in them would keep.

He found a blurry version of 'Schalcken the Painter' on a site he didn't want Mum to know he could access and watched the first ten minutes. It was nothing like 'The Cards'. The breakthrough was a bust.

If Little Angie read the *Radio Times* more carefully, would she have made her fuss about wanting to stay up late for this? It wasn't suitable for children because it was too boring. He skipped through and hit on a scene with an evil old man whose dead eyes gave him a chill. This might be distant kin to Mum's fear of the Holly Child.

He searched 'the cards' on IMDb and was offered only a stack of TV shows and films titled *House of Cards* and a Christian film called *The Miracle of the Cards* (2001). No help at all.

He input search terms.

Christmas ghost story the cards

Christmas ghost story not broadcast

Christmas ghost story imaginary

Note to Mum: next time, imagine something specific and unique. With a searchable key phrase. 'The Cards'? Ach. 'Schalcken the Painter' – that was easy to google.

He had no useful hits. The only faint trace online turned out to be an article by James Marion, Mum's uni not-boyfriend. 'British Folk Memory and Television Ghosts'. It covered the real Ghost Stories for Christmas – which seemed to have scared a lot of nervy nellies in the 1970s – but didn't stretch to 'The Cards', though Jamie was one of the few people Rust knew Mum had told about the imaginary story.

He fired off an email to the address on the academic site.

'Remember "The Cards"? New developments. Mum says "hi".' Jamie had visited Six Elms House several times and taken the trouble to have talks with him.

Jamie had left comments on the Paraphenomenon Pod board. He was the one who signalled that a rambler from Norfolk was passing off an M. R. James story about a whistle and a spectre on a beach as his own experience. The comment was at once helpful and annoying. Rust couldn't delete the whole episode but leaving it unmodified made him look like a credulous clot. He didn't thank Jamie for bringing the matter to his attention, but supposed he meant well.

Mum, centre of the universe, thought Jamie was interested in Rust because he wanted to keep open an option to be interested in her. She didn't get that Jamie and Rust had genuine overlaps in their fields of enquiry. Before the term 'Mandela Effect' caught on, Jamie wrote 'The Moonraker Effect', a paper based on a number of respondents who misremembered a joke from *Moonraker* as being better than it really was. Russell thought Jamie got gypped – the Moonraker Effect was a better name for the phenomenon. More shared false memories were about media – telly, films, songs, kids' books – than politicians.

He went to whatismymovie.com and input 'evil Christmas cards' as keywords. That gave him *The Devil's Brigade* (1968), *An All Dogs Christmas Carol* (1998) and *The Devil Rides Out* (1968). None fit the brief, though he watched most of *The Devil Rides Out* before powering off his tablet.

He still felt generally ropey. He was too exhausted by the cumulative worries of the last sixteen days to lie awake turning them over in his head. If he had nightmares, he didn't recall them after he woke up. He'd gone through a bad dreams phase when he was five or six but barely remembered what so frightened him. Not Bagpuss, certainly. He'd been disturbed by the acid green gunk that leaked from Mange the Schloup's batteries – and dreamed his own batteries were corroded and eating through his insides.

He dropped off.

Rooke descends from the sky to soft snow. He hasn't fully got the hang of flying yet but is drunk on stolen joy. He capers in his patch of garden, then sees today's card – number 17 – propped in the wreath. His cloak settles like deflated water-wings. He reaches for the card...

The shrub in the picture has become a little tree, with a twiggy, vaguely human shape. The robin is a stiff rotting corpse on its branch. The tree grows crookedly. It has come to fruit. Nut-like ornaments appear in its branches.

Eyes open among the pine needles.
Rooke bends over the firepit, in pain. He looks up at the cards and opens his mouth to scream. A leafy barb stabs his tonsils from his gullet. He looks at his hands. His nails are displaced by twigs growing inside his fingers.

No, it will not hold. It must not be. You're a ghost of a ghost, Master Christimas. Used up and done with and disposed of. I'll not be hampered by leftover pudding and such nonsense.

He tears the card in two but the halves reknit.

Cunning, but a mountebank's parlour trick.

He forces himself to stand straight.

∼

Rust woke in darkness. His bedside clock showed 04.14.

He was sure a noise had shaken him awake. A noise still lingering – not an echo, but a reverberation.

A volley of shots? More iciclequakes?

No – a rhythm, a drumbeat… *pa-rum-pa-pum-pum*.

By Great Gargantua, no!

Light came on outside his door. He slid out of bed and belted his dressing gown. He bumped into Mum on the landing. She wore men's pin-stripe pyjamas two sizes too big for her and hefted her burglar bludgeon – a rounders bat swollen with silver tape, kept by her bed after she did a ton of research into home invasions for a book and got paranoid.

'Did you hear…' he asked.

'Pa-rum-pa-pum-pum? Uh huh. Someone's getting pa-rum-pa-pum-pummelled.'

She swung the bludgeon and charged downstairs.

Rust followed.

The front door needed both of them to haul it open.

The forecourt was lit by the restrung illuminations. A coil of festive barbed wire wound around the mailbox. The flag was up. A curd of frost on the wooden roof looked like snow.

Rust looked down the Turn-Off but didn't see the lights of the Milk Float.

It couldn't have been more than a minute or so. The roof-bar should be visible through the thin hedges.

Thirty seconds outside at quarter past four in the morning was enough to freeze him through and through. The wind was like being sloshed in the face with ditch water. If his colon was filled with toxic stuffing, it turned into a coil of lumpy ice.

Mum handed him the bludgeon and hopped across the forecourt. She snatched the single offending item out of the mailbox and sprinted back. She got into the hallway and he shoved the door shut. They heard a click and a hiss…

The radiators came on this early. It took four hours to warm the house for human habitation.

Mum shivered like a hypothermia victim, shoulders shaking. Even indoors, her breath frosted. But she was focused on the card.

'Do you remember this one?' he asked.

She slit the envelope with his scalpel (so that's where it had got to).

'No,' she said, looking inside. 'Oh, wait. Yes. Yes, I do remember. Very funny. Hah.'

She showed it to him.

SEVENTEENTH NIGHT, WAKE IN FRIGHT…

'I'm digging that bear trap and setting an IUD.'

'IED.'

'I was being funny. Bitterly funny.'

'I know.'

'Can you go on the dark web and search "Explosive Devices – How to Improvise Them from Household Goods, Christmas Tree Decorations and Extra Mince Pie Mince"?'

He yawned, still tired.

The mention of mince pie mince gave him a pain. As if someone had crumbled a Christmas tree bauble into silvery splinters and worked them into the mince… knowing it would come to this.

Mum showed him the picture.

The Holly Child's krewe – zombie robin, a two-face angel, the manky militia and a compost heap with antlers – blotted out more of the trees. They were marching towards the front of the picture, as if advancing on a window or coming out of a screen. The star above was red as the robin's ripped-open chest.

He doubled over, clutching his stomach, using the bludgeon as a cane.

'Rust,' Mum said, alarmed.

He thought he'd be sick, but nothing came up. Whatever was inside him was rooted where it was.

Mum took him into the kitchen – the stone floor was an ice rink – and bent him over the sink. He could only produce a few snotty ropes of fluid. The quality of his pain shifted, as if organs usually oiled by blood or lymph were grinding together, dry as paper.

Then the cramp went away.

Mum looked very tired. He felt worn out.

But neither wanted to go back to sleep.

Angie stayed up the next night, alternating chapters of *Stabbing Sally-Anne* and *The Girl Who Got Ground Up*. She thought of camping in the lean-to on a garden chair. Even with three duvets and a Thermos of Baileys-laced coffee, she'd die of hypothermia. She stayed in the kitchen. With all the lights on, the window was an ebony mirror. Her reflection was a fright. With the overhead light off, Christmas sparkle was reflected but she could make out the mailbox. She clipped a pencil-torch to her blouse and aimed it at the page she was reading, looking up frequently to check the forecourt.

Night wasn't quite silent. Overriding the heating timer (damn the bills!) meant boiler burn and radiator hiss. But not a creature was stirring – except the nerveless, boneless flap of cold hand she used to turn the pages. Sally-Anne and the Girl took too long to get stabbed or ground up, so she couldn't recommend the books to her discerning readers. They wanted a corpse in the first chapter and regular twists thereafter.

No *pa-rum-pa-pum-pum* sounded.

04.14 came and went. She finished with the ARCs. Sally-Anne was an active stabber, not a passive stabbee – as Angie guessed early. The Girl survived the book without going into an industrial mincer because the grinder with a grudge liquidised her sister by mistake. Angie put the books on the table and burrowed deeper into her three-duvet nest. She rested her eyes…

∽

'Postman's been,' said Russell.

11.46. Blinding daylight. A cold cup of tea on the table, left by a considerate, loving son some hours earlier.

'And the turkey's here, delivered by a bloke who stopped and said hello and was normal.'

'Did you pay him?'

'Yes. That's why he stopped and said hello. Cash from the double decker bus tin. Was that right?'

'Yes.'

'Bird's in the fridge.'

'Good. Bring in the card?'

A hesitation. He'd waited for her to wake up.

Right.

She was settling this hash. She was a stabber, not a stabbee. She was not being ground up. What would Samantha do? Or Kathleen Turner?

She threw off her duvets and stood.

'Mum, what now?'

He followed her as she left the house.

The triffid growth in the woodpile was still a nuisance. Shoots poked through holes in the tarpaulin. She ignored the weed issue and considered the axes leaned against the wall – the small one for kindling, the medium one for splitting logs and the big one for chopping down trees. There were no elms left to chop down at Six Elms so she'd never needed the big axe. She'd bought the full set because of a three for two offer.

Deep down, maybe she'd known one day she'd need the big axe.

She hefted it and got a feel of the weight. If the Holly Child was coming for Russell, she wasn't going to respect the Geneva Convention.

'Watch out, Mum,' said her son.

She marched round to the front of the house and took a run-up across the forecourt, then executed the swing she'd practised with the burglar bludgeon in case a stalker tracked her down...

The blade sliced through the model house and wedged in the baseboard.

The mailbox was thoroughly smashed. She had to lever the axe free before taking a swipe at the supporting pole. The fairy lights sparked out and the pole got knocked over – though not sheared through or completely unstuck from its hole. She gave the thing a few more Lizzie Borden whacks for good measure.

'Let's see how you deliver cards when there's nowhere to deliver to!'

She had a guilt-sorrow twinge. She'd liked that mailbox.

Eric had made sweet Little Angie and Russell figures to stand on front of the house. They had only escaped Angelica Axe by being on temporary loan to the Christmas tree. *Angelica Axe* was a possible title. She'd run it past Jerzy to find out what it was in Polish.

'I said the post had been, Mum,' said Russell.

In the wreck, undamaged, was today's card. '18'.

Russell picked it out and opened it.

'"Ten and eight, 'ware thy fate",' she said.

He looked at the message.

'Yep,' he said.

Ten and eight, 'ware thy fate

'It's like Evil Bingo now,' she said.

Angie didn't want to look at the picture but saw it all the same. The uprooted Holly Child filled the middle of the image. Its chest hung with ornaments. Glistening sap trickled from pinpricks. Its mates crowded around. Robin Deadbreast with spread wings. Toy Soldiers had fixed bayonets.

'You were half-right when you tried to take them to the recycle bin,' she said. 'We should burn the bastards.'

'No,' he insisted, holding the card to his chest. 'Not before we get an answer. We need to solve the mystery.'

'We're a long way past podcat grist now. When the crocodile

gets too close, you toss the camera and run. You're not David Attenborough any more… you're din-dins.'

She wasn't getting through to him. He swallowed pain.

'Nothing's actually happened, Mum. Just cards. I know what they are. A recognised paraphenomenon. They are apports. Things which materialise. Usually stones or pins or small nubbins. Bleed-through from other planes of reality…'

Angie couldn't believe her son.

'Rust, here's a secret,' she told him. 'At some point, every mystery story turns into a horror story.'

```
Rokesby Roylott Village Green on a December
morn.

Beadle Bramblebush, dressed as Father
Christmas, sits in a rustic grotto and pulls
presents from a sack for the excited children
of the parish. Grown-up villagers quaff
mulled wine and indulgently watch youths
toss snowballs at each other around a huge,
communal-effort snowman.

A dark figure - Rooke - approaches the grotto.
A stray snowball flies towards him. He catches
it like a cricket ball. He squeezes hard,
smiles nastily, and drops what has become a
lump of coal.

The child who flung the snowball is horror-
struck.

Rooke gets a hit of stolen joy. He extends
psychic tendrils which latch onto everyone
here.
```

Bramblebush goes from plump and merry to
shrivelled and fear-struck. His beard falls
away to show a haggard face. The grotto
crumbles around him.

Rooke laughs lustily.

Children scream. Gifts fall in the snow.
Adults wail. A lost hoop, partially wrapped,
rolls away and falls over.

Rooke is replete with joy. The green is
littered with broken people, mostly not dead
but in trauma and despair.

Rooke makes a conjuration, and the snowman
melts - becoming the village pond.

Rooke looks to the reddish horizon. Sees the
serrated shadows of the treetops of a pine
forest.

They lurch - the forest marches towards the
village.

Hah, be you still nuisance, Master Christimas...
but of no matter, no concern and no threat.

Rooke rises, robes spreading like dark
wings. Bubo baubles on his chest glow like
candleflames.

∽

Woodland scene. Robin. Snow. Star.

The bleeding robin screams. A greyish, shambling lump of
a snowman barges between trees. The Merciless Gentlemen

gather in its tracks. Jingle Basterds All the Way. The star is veiled with blood. A snow smile becomes a grin. Egg-yolk eyes, with blood swirling in them. An angry Christmas tree bursts out from inside the snowman. It was the Tree Ghost all the time. Meet the Holly Child.

Rust had taken digital photos. A click-through gallery turned the cards into a short clip. He looked at it on his tablet.

With his big present – hidden in the disused bread oven, like it was every year – he could make actual animation. Next year was going to be all about the pivot to video. A lot of pods were going that route – shorter episodes, with image collages, film clips, to-camera spiel and video interviews. Perry and Skye were there already – but they'd have nothing like this to show for their home studio. An animation made from apports.

He reclicked through the gallery.

It was too short to put music to. Maybe menacing bells?

Could sleigh-bells really be menacing? In the proper context, yes.

He reclicked again. It was different every time, depending on which day's card held the screen for a few seconds longer.

He searched 'menacing bells', which turned out to be a cassette album by an artist called Noise Nomads.

Like he could make his toe or tummy or back hurt by thinking of it, he could fool his ears. He heard menacing bells. Not from his tablet.

> *On the first day of Christmas,*
> *my true love sent to me…*
> *a death threat in a pear tree!*

The voice was high, a little girlish.
Was his mum singing a Christmas Cruel somewhere…

On the second day of Christmas,
my true love sent to me
two poison pills…
and a death threat in a pear tree!

'Ho flaming ho,' said Russell.

On the third day of Christmas
my true love sent to me
three dirty bombs,
two poison pills…
and a death threat in a pear tree!

Rust rolled his chair back from his bedside desk and stood.
His room had a low ceiling. He couldn't hang models from
it any more because he'd bump his head.
    Where was the singing coming from?

On the fourth day of Christmas
my true love sent to me
four falling bricks,
three dirty bombs,
two poison pills…
and a death threat in a pear tree!

If this was Perry and Skye, he'd denial-of-service Peasons
in a pod to oblivion. North Korean hackers weren't the equal
of Wrathful Rust Wickings.

Did the song come from inside the wall?

He opened his wardrobe. He used to make his G-bot Base in it, beneath the hanging coats. Nestled in the site of many imagined mecha-on-monster battles was a pale child in a pinafore dress and grubby trainers. She looked up, wearing his own face.

He shut the door, quickly.

Silence. No more presents from anyone's true love.

It was cold in his room, despite the space heater. But he was sweating.

He was not frightened. Just surprised.

Had he seen a ghost? He had.

He should have expected it, eventually. He'd put his head over the parapet with his pod. Every episode dropped was like waving a light in a chasm. Whatever was out there would take notice eventually and start swimming through the darkness towards him.

He opened the door again. No little girl.

Drat. Had he lost it? Lost her?

He was already questioning what he'd definitely seen.

Could he have shaped a little girl out of fallen-down coats and the mirror at the back of the wardrobe? He used to imagine a portal there.

Scientifically, what to do? Summoning through sacrifice was in made-up stories. He couldn't think of anything to offer anyway. Maybe ritual chanting – a mantra – would do the trick? The manifestation was primarily auditory. He still didn't quite believe in the pivot to video.

Thanks to Mum, he knew the song…

'On the fifth day of Christmas my true love sent to me… *five old things*… four falling bricks, three dirty bombs, two poison pills… and a death threat in a pear tree!'

He waited. Then, distant, did he hear or was he singing in his head...?

> *On the sixth day of Christmas*
> *my true love sent to me*
> *six guns a-shooting,*
> *five old things,*
> *four falling bricks,*
> *three dirty bombs,*
> *two poison pills...*
> *and a death threat in a pear tree!*

Call and response. He sang. She sang.

> *'... seven shanks a-shanking.'*
> *... eight thugs a-thumping.*
> *'... nine lasers slicing.'*
> *... ten cords a-strangling.*

There was back and forth. The ghost was not recorded on the stone tape... not pictures in a book. The duet meant she was a person – a personality. He was sceptical of discarnate survival of personality. Ghosts were winter coats left behind when the traveller moved on to places like summer. Or shaped echoes in reality, like worm-casts in the earth. Ghosts were not people.

> *'... eleven snipers sniping.'*

The singing was wordless now, approximating the tune – it didn't sound like a little girl, but like an animal mimicking a child, or wind through a flute. More like his idea of a ghost.

It should be

'twelve killers killing'…

The song changed almost every time. It had been made up by Grandad with help from Mum, then changed by Mum with help from Rust. In one version, the true love gifts were monster threats and Gargantuabots. That tailored-to-seven-year-old-Russell cruel was seldom heard now. The classic words were back.

The noise continued. More like bells than whistles. A ringing in his head? No, it was coming from inside the wardrobe.

He unplugged his digital camera from his tablet.

This would be the video to get. If it were gettable.

Gingerly, he opened the wardrobe again. No apparent child, but her nest was here and the mirror out of place. *Was* there a portal back there? Like the way to Narnia. He'd looked for holes in time and space when he wondered whether Six Elms was a paraphen locus, and been disappointed. Portals, unlike physical doors, came and went, though. Apports came through portals sometimes.

Camera up, he ducked under the lintel and pushed in among the coats.

The door shut behind him. The only light in the dark was the red recording indicator on the camera.

Were the menacing bells giggling?

So, a personality, then. Not a nice personality.

∽

Presuming a muffled noise indicated welcome, Angie opened Russell's bedroom door. She'd made thick cocoa. Not a tonic for whatever he was coming down with, like the Lemsip Mum had given her when she was poorly, but a psychic pick-me-up. A drug in cocoa made you happy. Goosing the brain rallied the body. It was science.

Russell's tablet was open and the room felt like there was a person in it. But her son wasn't to be seen. Turning invisible must count as a paraphenomenon. She hoped he wasn't experimenting. In stories, invisible men all went mad.

The wardrobe door opened from the inside.

She should have considered a rational solution before scrolling down to the helm of invisibility option.

Russell bumped his head extricating himself.

'So you're coming out of the closet?'

'That'd be easier to explain,' he said.

'I should cocoa. Speaking of beverages suitable for just-before-bedtime…'

She handed him the mug.

The image on his tablet caught her eye. The Holly Child, ready to pounce. Yellow eyes narrowing. Ice breathed on the back of her neck. Then she saw the image was still. Russell had photographed the cards. This was not a digighost pushing its face into the real world.

Maybe they shouldn't have watched *The Ring*?

She picked up the tablet and looked at those yellow eyes.

'Mum, digital privacy act!'

Angie handed his tablet over.

Russell checked his precious to make sure the parental touch hadn't bricked it. Then he came at her sideways and sly, working up to something.

'Mum, this was your bedroom, wasn't it?'

She still thought it the most comforting, safest room in the house – though no matter what you did with a space heater it was too cold this time of year.

'Yes,' she admitted. 'This was me when I was little. I had *way* cooler posters. David Bowie on that wall. And Gary Glit— come to think of it, your *Gargantuabots Go Go Go* quad is a valued collectable.'

'Did you ever see or hear anything in this room?'

'Um, yes – abled person here.'

'Anything paraphenomenal?'

'Spooky, you mean? No. We knew all about the village's reputation. Sutton Mallet was overrun with ghost hunters every October. Pete Peason was one of them. The twins get it from him.'

'Here, at Six Elms, in this room. Did you feel... I don't know, *watched*?'

'No, Rust, I was convinced *everywhere else* was haunted. The old stable at Daintry Farm where Janet Speke told me Dick Turpin hanged himself *and his horse*. The bricked-up fireplace in the kitchen where the evil stuffed cat lived. That bend in the Cut-Off where you can be surprised by someone walking the other way. But my room was out of bounds. Here was home safe. Even under the bed. No ghosts allowed. It's a good policy. You should adopt it.'

Russell sipped his cocoa. He didn't scald his lip.

'There'll be another card tomorrow,' he said.

'There will,' she admitted. '"Nineteen, nineteen, know what I mean?" No – "Two tens less one, you'll not have fun". I can't remember.'

Russell kept sipping. He had a cocoatache. It made him look suave but vulnerable.

'One thing, though,' she said.

'What?'

'It'll be over by Christmas.'

```
A log fire in the hearth at Wychward Cottage.
A strew of cards among the flames, refusing
to catch light.

Ill-tempered, Rooke hovers close to the fire -
not for warmth, but to watch the spell.

A puff of red smoke. Rooke coughs. The fire
is out.

Eighteen cards are arranged on the shelf above
the fire. Rooke looks at them. Something - a
rat? a homunculus? - moves behind the cards,
shaking them.

Rooke takes cards away and puts them back as
if playing 'Find the Lady'.

He doesn't find anything. He looks at his
hands, and finds his fingers sheathed with
frost.

Pah! And hah! And Bug-Hum!
```

∽

Sutton Mallet was playing tricks again.

According to the BBC, it was unseasonably warm across the South-West: 14 degrees at Burnham-on-Sea and 16.3 in Sedgwater, a record high for December. According to the kitchen window, silent snow had fallen in the night. Six Elms was blanketed. The Cut-Off was a winding river of unbroken drifts. The forecourt was a virgin field, sparkling and slightly blue like a spilled lorryload of washing powder. The recycling bin and the lean-to wore thick fluffy caps.

Under it all, earth would be hard as iron, water like a stone.

Angie knew conditions wouldn't deter the card deliverer.

If needs be, the Milk Float could be replaced by a drone.

The curse would get through.

Dad had devised an emergency routine. Twice when she was little, Six Elms got snowed in – once during a supposed summer heatwave which turned the rest of the county yellow. It was worse than being cut off by floods. Electricity went out, frozen pipes burst, supplies ran low. I Spy was always something beginning with S. Dad, Mum and Angie had to play board games. Dad would make up new rules so he'd win.

She still remembered which pipes to hit with a hammer.

Russell flushed the upstairs and downstairs loos and checked taps in the bathroom and kitchen. Free flow. Warm water. Praise the plumbing.

Dad had cladded and secured danger point joints. Angie went mist-eyed. Dad had been gone eight years now, but his cladding held. He didn't need to haunt Six Elms. He'd done his best when he was alive. The candles and matches he'd bought were still in the doomsday stash, though she'd replaced the bottled water and muesli bars. It would take more than snowmageddon to get Russell to eat a muesli bar.

House operational, they had to venture outside. To check gutters and tiles.

The front door was a trial. It was too heavy and scraped across flagstones. A seal of ice needed cracking. A drift tumbled into the hallway and had to be swept back. The air was still so they didn't get a chilling blast in their faces… just felt creeping ambient cold settling in their bones. They wrapped up in padded coats and put on stout wellies.

Russell put Neil Armstrong boot prints on the steps. She had to be Buzz Aldrin.

The crouching stones were buried. If there was lore about reducing the effectiveness of household wards by dumping half a hundredweight of snowflakes on them, she didn't want to download a podcast about it.

'Mum, this isn't right,' said Russell, stepping carefully onto the forecourt.

'Absolute-a-mente, Rust. Sixteen point three my arse…'

'It's like…'

'Climate catastrophe, yes. An extreme weather event. I knew we should have started recycling earlier.'

She followed him, treading in his bootsteps.

On top of the lean-to was a ghost-shaped hump. Inside was a fat plastic robin, its lit-up redbreast glowing through a snow-shell.

Green weed swarmed around the corner of the house. It climbed the wall. Seed-sacs had split. She bet the berries would be poison.

'It's like a Christmas card,' said Russell.

In place of the trashed mailbox stood an old-fashioned snowman. Buttons for eyes, carrot nose, knitted scarf – as if posing for the cover of a vintage double issue of the *Radio Times*. The work of Mr Pa-Rum-Pa-Pum-Pum?

Sliced into the snowman's head like an axe-blade was today's card.

'Let's leave it,' said Russell. 'We might break the cycle.'

She was tempted but had to go through with it.

Two tens less one, Yule begun.

'What's the picture?'

She showed him.

'Big evil Christmas tree, what else? The Holly Child is coming for you.'

He was looking at the ground around the snowman. No footprints, of course.

The fields were snowed under as far as they could see. But the skies were clear. They might as well be inside a snow globe.

Any visitors they would have before the New Year were already here.

⁓

Today's card was on the mantelpiece. The Holly Child had shaken off most of its snow-shell. It looked like what Mum said it was. An angry Christmas tree.

Rust found himself avoiding the real tree in case it went feral.

They set up again in the sitting room.

A fire was going in the grate. They'd decided not to burn the weed and had to hack firewood free from its webbing. Cut, the weed gave off a sweet smell. Cinnamon toast. He now tasted cinnamon in his spittle. The stuff inside had stopped giving him gyp, like a symbiote coming to terms with its host – calculating how slowly to feed, to delay the moment when the parasite strangled its unwitting landlord and had to move on. But he was weaker than he used to be. He had to rest after going up or down stairs. He reckoned he couldn't get more than a dozen yards on his bike, even under ideal conditions.

Just thinking about cycling gave him chill sweats.

Hooking his tablet up to the enormoscreen was a complex procedure, but worth it. He had hopes for this call. James Marion had emailed back wanting to talk with them. Maybe he'd help.

Jamie wasn't free until late afternoon. Faculty drinks he couldn't get out of. Mum said he would probably be sozzled in a paper hat. Lipstick kisses on his cheeks from loitering under mistletoe. Mum made Jamie out to be a cartoon character.

But she'd put on her author photo outfit and make-up for the Skype call.

She sat up in a chair rather than slumped on the sofa. Tummy in, chest out.

Rust sat cross-legged by the low table, with his tablet, the TV remote and a back-up audio recorder in front of him. A webcam was propped on the rim of the enormoscreen.

'I'm not sure I can take post-faculty drinks Jamie in hi-def,' said Mum.

A bit too bright and sparkly. She had nerves again.

Mum and Jamie had history. But not, as she said, geography – since uni, they'd never lived in the same county. She had a degree in English Lit and thought Media Studies wasn't a real subject. She kept up with Jamie the way he kept up with her books but hadn't noticed his pivot to hauntology. He was a professor, but she still thought of him as the mature student she met on a train to a poll tax demo in 1990. She didn't get arrested that time, but the next day – April the First – she'd phoned Jamie's brother Keith and told him Jamie was in the nick for punching a policeman. It had, apparently, been hilarious, though it took Keith a while to see the funny side.

16.10. Time to Skype.

Rust used the remote to turn on the enormoscreen. His

tablet display was blown up. His Gretelgeuse in a Bikini wallpaper was studded with shortcut icons.

He clicked into Skype.

He should have done prep upstairs. Three women with Russian names wanted to start conversations with him. He blocked them while his mother made snarky comments about them looking nice and friendly.

'Everyone gets these, Mum,' he said.

'You can chat up Svetlana, Irina and Countess Spatula later, dear. Get tips about how to stay warm in snow…'

Jamie logged on from an academic server.

Mum patted her hair and adjusted her blouse. She wore a brooch Russell thought Jamie had given her.

There he was. Professor Marion, in his office, wearing a Christmas jumper. His face was at the bottom of the screen. Too much ceiling above him. Good thing Russell was only recording audio.

Jamie had a much better picture of Mum than they had of him.

He angled his laptop camera so at least his chin was in the frame. Behind him was a framed poster for *Quatermass and the Pit*.

'Angelle,' said Jamie, 'you're there. You look… you, as usual. And hello, Russell…'

'Rust. He's called Rust.'

'Of course he is. This is about "The Cards" isn't it?'

'You remember?' Mum was a bit surprised.

'The file's still open.'

'Jamie did research,' Mum told Russell. 'Before archives were all online.'

'It's easy to find out what was broadcast, Rust,' said Jamie. 'It's tricky to prove that something *wasn't*. Had to check listings for every channel your house could have received... "Viewers in Wales have their own programmes".'

'We were tuned to the wrong BBC,' Mum told Rust, for about the hundredth time. 'The *Radio Times* would promise cartoons and you'd switch on to get a farming programme in Welsh.'

'Did you find anything?' Russell asked.

'Well, not nothing. The first thing we established was that in 1979 the BBC stopped doing their annual Christmas Ghost Story. No one agrees why. Too popular, possibly. Or complaints from the Mary Whitehouse Brigade. They did sneak in "Schalcken the Painter", however.'

'The Sheridan Le Fanu story?' asked Mum.

Jamie nodded.

'There's a telly of "Schalcken"?'

'It was on the night before Christmas Eve, Mum,' Rust said.

'An episode of *Omnibus*,' Jamie said.

'The boring arts programme?'

'Yes, though I'd disagree about boring,' said Jamie. 'Jonathan Miller's "Whistle and I'll Come to You" was an *Omnibus*. That started the M. R. James craze at the BBC, in 1968. I'm surprised you didn't notice the Le Fanu film.'

'Too busy going mad, apparently.'

Jamie half-smiled whenever Mum snarked at him. He sat back to suppress a flinch, then leaned forward to plough on with what he wanted to say.

'Did you consider BSI?' Rust asked.

'We – I – thought of that too. Park the theory for a bit. Have you come across thoughtography?'

'Also known as psychic photography, projected thermography, nengraphy...'

'... and *nensha* in Japanese.'

Mum made a thumb-across-the-throat gesture.

'Not so fast, parageeks. Explanation needed for the lay person here.'

Jamie calmed down and spoke less like an enthusiast at a Fortean symposium and more like someone delivering an 'introduction to…' lesson.

'I wouldn't have considered thoughtography when you told me about "The Cards" in 1990. It's fringy even now. Some gifted people, supposedly, can burn mental images onto film. It used to be still photographs. Rorschach shapes. Wavy lines, stars and so on. More and more cases involve moving images. Like a television programme that doesn't exist.'

Mum was losing patience. She always did with Jamie. It was embarrassing.

'Jamie, if I could make a TV show with my mind, do you think I'd be self-publishing? I'd project a streaming series with Angelina Jolie and Tom Cruise and coin it in.'

'It would explain a lot,' Rust put in, trying to stick up for Jamie.

'It explains nothing. Jamie – you're a *terrible* influence. How's Carol?'

Jamie pushed on…

'There's something else, Angelle. Even before Rust got in touch, I thought of putting a note in your Christmas card.'

'Which we haven't received. We've mostly had cards from Hell this year.'

Jamie was about to say something. Mum was even about to listen.

He opened his mouth…

The power went out. The enormoscreen died. Rust's tablet, on 17 per cent battery, faded. The Skype connection cut as the

Wi-Fi died. The tree lights went off. The LEDs on a stack of devices went dark. Red light came from the fire.

While they were on the call, night had fallen. It was as if the outsides of the windows were painted black.

'Bugger!' said Mum.

◠

The eyes of the Holly Child on the cards gleamed yellow. They must be dabs of luminous paint.

Dad's doomsday stash was open. They had enough candles, but not enough candlesticks. Angie used egg cups as substitutes. It was ages since anyone at Six Elms boiled an egg for breakfast.

She thought about putting candles on the mantelpiece.

Maybe the cards would catch fire.

She propped two candles on the windowsill. The flames waved at doppelgangers in the glass. Between candle- and firelight, the sitting room was almost cosy – though if the supply of dry logs ran out, duvet-cloaks would be a necessity. The tree, a sorry thing with its illuminations out, stretched spidery shadows up the wall and across the ceiling. Baubles tinkled whenever anyone came into the room... and could be heard from the hallway when it was supposed to be empty.

Russell's tablet was frozen – battery at 4 per cent. He watched it die rather than turn it off.

Back to the dark ages...

'We'll have to make our own entertainment,' she said.

'Are you sure that's a good idea, Mum? First time you made your own entertainment, it led to this... haunting.'

'Hah. We're beyond paraphenomena then? Without Wi-Fi, it's a haunting. Something old and crafty in the woods

117

projected "The Cards" onto the telly or into my head… now it's thoughtographing a remake with CGI and a higher body count?'

Russell had been warming up to confide – or confess – something. Skyping with Poor Old Jamie had been a diversion.

'There's an apparition,' he said. 'A girl.'

'Yes, like Tatiana and Svetlana and those bunny hussies. Now *you're* dreaming spirits into reality.'

'Not that kind of girl. A little girl.'

'A *ghost*?'

Russell didn't want to say the word.

Angie was about to ask if the little girl was in the room with them now but nipped the thought. She might not like the answer.

'She knows the Death Threat Christmas Cruel. So she's from around here…'

'"On the first day of Christmas",' sang Angie, '"my true love sent to me"…'

'… "a death threat in a pear tree." Yes.'

In candlelight, Russell looked younger. Not fifteen. Five.

'Where've you been hiding this little madam?' she said. 'Do we know her parents?'

He smiled, with pain.

'She's not what we should worry about. She's a familiar.'

'You what?'

'An attendant demon. Like the cats witches have. A warm-up act. She makes minor mischief… but something serious comes after her. To do real damage.'

'Where are you getting all this?'

'You, Mum.'

Russell took a copy of *Warlock Wendy* off the shelf. The one she always liked to forget about. Jerzy's favourite, funnily enough? Though it didn't do well in Poland either.

'Yes,' she admitted, 'as you now know, I plagiarised my childhood nightmare for my least successful book. What of it?'

She'd vaguely hoped readers might recognise something in *Warlock Wendy* and explain it to her. Only there hadn't been enough readers to furnish useful leads.

'You keep leaving clues even you don't notice, Mum.'

She took her own book and flicked through it. She'd tipped in chunks of 'The Cards' – everything, in fact, but the cards. In her grown-up version, Wendy Rooke got away with it. She sucked joy out of a gated community in Surrey and splurged it away at a carnival in Rio de Janeiro.

'You're a mystery-solver, Rust. You take the fun out of everything.'

Russell indicated the mantelpiece and its row of yellow eyes.

'Call this fun?'

'Of a sort.'

He kept rolling back his sleeve to check the time. He didn't often wear the digital watch Horst had given him. Usually, multiple screens with date/time displays were in easy eyeshot. The watch was a comfort now.

Devices still worked. The power would be back.

'It's nearly midnight,' he said. 'How long till the next card?'

'I don't know, love. Supernatural curse delivery isn't what it was before Brexit.'

$\sim$

From the window on the upstairs landing, Rust surveilled the snowscape with Grandad's binoculars. He scoped out the snowman. No card was sliced into its head. It seemed less a made thing today, more like an accident – an unusual drift misread by the eye. The face had fallen and the scarf was gone.

The power wasn't back – so no central heating, no space heater, no hot water.

He wore gloves and a scarf indoors.

Six Elms House had fireplaces in the kitchen and sitting room and enough wood to last till spring. They had a morning session with axes. Christmas weed had to be hacked away so they could get to the woodpile. Using the small axe on the weed spilled sap and made him taste cinnamon again. Mum split logs and Rust chopped kindling. She said the activity would warm them up. In fact, it made him sweaty. With no hot water, he couldn't shower.

He was clumsy and after a few minutes' exertion his head was swimming. Mum was too worried to rib him for the poor job he did of the kindling. He couldn't grip the hatchet properly or aim at wood propped a few inches away. Eventually, she said he'd hurt himself if he carried on and took the small axe away.

Grandad's doomsday stash included a camping stove. They could boil water for tea and coffee – and eggs, though the cups were in use – and heat canned soup to have with bread and cheese. Mince pies with any amount of mince were running low.

When night fell – one day short of the longest night of the year, so just after lunch – candles were distributed around the habitable parts of the house.

In the hallway, Rust found an envelope on the mat.

The letterbox was inconveniently low in the front door. It hadn't been used since Eric's mailbox was put up to save

Post-Lady Petal from clumping across the forecourt and bending down.

Because the door opened inwards and scraped flagstones, there usually wasn't a mat inside. Mum had put it there so they could stamp snow off their wellies without tramping too much into the house.

'Mum,' he called.

Sitting on the stairs was the little girl Mum didn't believe in. The apparition – familiar – manifestation – ghost-adjacent paraphenomenon. Her face pressed between banisters like a prisoner's between bars.

Was he seeing things? Hallucinating, daydreaming or misreading? A duvet hung over the banisters, fetched from the unused, fridge-like spare room. It had faces on it. Not a little girl's but a 1920s cartoon party. Flappers with cigarette holders and handsome sketchy men with cocktails. Looked at again, the faces might fit together into a puzzle picture of a sitting child. Or not. Just now, he wouldn't take a floating sheet with eyeholes at face value.

A candle came out of the kitchen. Mum's face floated towards him – more ghostly than the apparition he thought might actually be a ghost.

'Look,' he said, pointing.

'Delivered by drone,' she said. 'Or robin.'

She picked it up and gave it to him.

Two and oh, tides of woe...

The card had an extra fold, making the woodland scene panoramic. The Holly Child was out of its snowy shell and

turned into a warrior tree, backed by a crowd of Christmas
bruisers. The Merciless Gentlemen and the Jingle Basterds.

'Tomorrow, we'll have him,' Mum swore. 'Poison Postman
Pat.'

Twenty-one cards on the mantel.

Rooke, bloated from his last meal, stands in
his cold firepit. His sorcerer's robe parts
over his sunken chest. Pine needles grow out
of his skin. Apple-red buboes swell around his
neck. Mistletoe lumps in his side-whiskers.

*'Shortest day, time to pray...' Pray, eh? Pray
to whom? To what? Diabolus. Satani. Herne. I
defy thee, Father Christimas... you are dead
and done and have holly through you. All this
is but an inconvenient residue. One more meal
of pure joy - Christimas joy, with presents
- and you'll be stick-dry and forgotten.
Magister Rooke will have had the best of it,
the best of the season.*

Last thing at night, Mum nailed an offcut across the letterbox.

First thing in the morning, they were up and ready.

Mum suggested Rust put on his Gargantuastrikeforce
armour, but it was Age 3–8 and didn't fit any more. He made
do with his Gargantuabot Rex helmet. Now suitable for indoor
wear. He'd forgotten what it was like not to be cold.

She gave him the burglar bludgeon but kept the big axe.

He checked the time. 09.08. His watch still felt like a
clanking bracelet.

'It's past nine,' he said. 'Shouldn't it be light?'

No sunlight penetrated the hallway.

'December the Twenty-First,' she said. 'Shortest day.'

'Yes, no, but…'

'No yes-no-butting in the ranks,' she barked. 'Great Gargantua tolerates no yes-no-butting…'

'Yes. No. But…'

Mum worried him. Scared him, almost. Laying it on too thick wasn't the half of it. If she were on a downslope, he could adjust and put up with it. The mood swings were doing his nut. Barking Sergeant-Major one moment… Granny Gloom 'N' Doom the next… you never knew what was behind today's window.

Mood swings were the first sign anything was wrong with Red Rudiger.

Lights outside. Not the sun.

'Do you hear what I hear?' asked Mum.

Rust strained his ears. With no radiator hiss or device hums, the house wasn't silent. Sounds you couldn't hear normally were there – creaky boards, wind-whistles, icicle drips. Something else – like throats being cleared.

Then music…

Yes, he heard what she heard…

Away in a manger,
no crib for a bed…
the little Lord Jesus
lay down his sweet head…

A carol concert. A radio – or a choir on the doorstep? Or was it in their minds? EVP with harmonies.

...the stars in the night sky
looked down where he lay...
the little Lord Jesus
asleep in the hay...

Mum pointed at the door and nodded him forward.

...the cattle are lowing,
the baby awakes...
but little Lord Jesus
no crying he makes...

He put the bludgeon aside and gripped the knob with both hands.

'If you wind up putting an axe in a vicar's skull, don't say I didn't warn you,' he said.

Mum shook her head. 'That's not real carol singing. It's another kind of Christmas Cruel.'

The door shrieked as he wrenched it open.

The angelic choir shut up.

A white wall filled the doorway, almost to the top – leaving a sliver of thin, spoiled-milk daylight.

'Gargantuabots, go go go!' shouted Mum.

She chopped her axe at the wall. The white wasn't packed ice but piled snow. It gave no resistance. The axe disappeared into the snow like a hot spoon in trifle. She lost hold of the handle.

Pa-rum-pa-pum-pum.

As if posted into a pillar box, a card popped through the sliver of light and flew into the hall like a paper plane.

SHORTEST DAY, TIME TO PRAY...

In the picture, the Holly Child and the Jingle Basterds had scarves and hats and hymn-sheets. The wooden sergeant-major held a lantern on a pole. Their mouths were open in Os of ululation. They weren't carollers. They were curse-chanters, putting the Wickingses of Six Elms House on notice.

No quarter, no mercy – and a happy New Year.

∽

Angie sat in her kitchen. She wore a dressing gown over two jumpers, thermals, a tracksuit and several pairs of socks.

After experimenting with available headwear, it turned out the Santa hat with fur trim – worn two years ago when posing for her own non-cursed cards – was the only one in the house that satisfactorily covered her ears. So, here she was looking Christmassy, when she'd rather the holiday were struck from the calendar. Cromwell had the right idea and banned celebrations.

She exhaled just to see her breath form droplets. It was like the last scene of *The Thing* – Jamie Marion's favourite film – inside the house. Was her son human? Was she? Who could know? Temperature dropping, doomsday imminent.

'We should make an inventory of perishables,' said Russell.

He was being practical today. Which was maddening and mad.

He opened the big fridge. The light didn't go on, of course. It was still packed with goodies. Cheese, chocolate and bacon jammed in around the turkey. The bird took up too much space.

'I shouldn't worry about anything spoiling,' she said. 'It's colder out than it would be inside a working fridge.'

Russell prodded the turkey with a forefinger. A greasy patch of skin slid away.

'Turkey's off,' he said.

She could smell it from where she was. She got up and walked over to look.

Between them, they extracted the bird from the fridge. Slippery from meltwater, it glistened with rot. Under the skin, the meat was greenish and scaly. They dumped the turkey on the big table as if for dissection. She remembered the defibrillator scene in *The Thing* and giggled.

'What, Mum?'

'Nothing. Just a bit from a film.'

Even left out in the open, the bird shouldn't have spoiled so quickly.

'It's haunted,' she said.

'Mum?' His voice was a bit squeaky.

'It's what you want, isn't it?' she said. 'You and Jamie. A paraphenomenon. Podcat fodder. A thoughtographed anomaly. Suitable for analysis. Not crazy. Not a mess. Not a catastrophe.'

She sounded shrill even to her own muffled ears.

Why was she like this? Microaggressive to the max.

She went back to exhaling frost shapes.

'Mum, you can't just say "it's haunted" and sit down again. These are things that are happening which we have to deal with. Like bad weather, like a power cut.'

'Both of which your haunting has delivered in the run-up to Christmas.'

Little Angie wanted a ghost story late at night on Christmas Eve and got one. Mid-sized Rust wanted paraphenomena to podcast about. Here they were, on a plate. Sutton Mallet gave the Wickingses the Christmas presents they asked for.

'We were cut off by floods. You said we had power cuts before. This is just that, with bells on.'

'Those were things that happened which weren't aimed at us specifically. They weren't out to get us. This so very much is.'

She took a long prong and stuck it in the turkey. It bled green sap.

She smelled cinnamon.

Jerzy said in Poland they had carp instead of turkey, kept live in the bath until Christmas Eve. If they'd done that, the fish would have evolved legs and be terrorising Six Elms like one of Gretelgeuse's monster threats.

'We need to be prepared, like Grandad planned,' said Russell. 'We need coping stratagems. Work-arounds. A checklist.'

Sympathy bubbled up inside her. She laid a mittened hand on her son's shoulder. 'Charlie Chen's sweet and sour for Christmas dinner?' she suggested. 'With prawn crackers?'

'Absolutely,' he said. 'If that's what it takes. Crispy fried sprouts. Fortune cookies with sixpences inside.'

Then he looked sick. He often looked sick now.

'Have you eaten something off? Please tell me you've not sneaked slices off this turkey.'

He sat down, carefully – as if trying not to rupture himself.

'It was that advent calendar chocolate,' he said. 'On the first day of Christmas. The death threat in a pear tree. A magic bean. It's sprouted.'

'From little acorns, mighty oaks...'

'It's not an oak,' he said, through gritted teeth. 'It's an evergreen.'

His face twisted. The spasm passed and he was calm again.

Which perked her up no end. Cinnamon – yumm. There was some in the spice rack.

'You aren't well, poor love,' she said. 'A day or two in bed, perhaps. I'll make cocoa. With a secret extra ingredient.'

She winked at him.

Her son looked at her as if she were mad.

He often did. But usually as if she were harmlessly mad – going barefoot in a muddy field, or talking back to Boris Johnson on the telly, or making up rude words to Christmas Number Ones and calling them Christmas Number Twos. Now, he looked at her as if she were an axe-murderess with the heads of three old boyfriends in her fridge – Christmas goodies jammed in around their ears and chins, and spice-scented candles burning to cover the stench.

First thing next day, she checked the front door. Still shut against a mountain of snow. The big axe was lost until the spring thaw. She shoved the welcome mat against the door-crack. Nothing could get through.

In the sitting room, she experimentally toggled a light-switch.

No joy.

Against hope, she patted the radiator. Cold.

So it was still 1850 at Six Elms. Fine, Magister Rooke. Should that be how thee wantst to play fiddle-de-dee, then Mistress Wickings be more'n a match for 'ee, I dare say and say I dare. Harrumph and Bug-Hum!

The grate held yesterday's ashes and embers. Not many logs piled by the hearth. An expedition out the back door would have to fetch wood. The Christmasweed would have to be hacked away. She didn't believe it grew from a putrid County Stores chocolate. It was a hybrid of horror holly, poison ivy and murder mistletoe.

Tomorrow's logs should be piled by today's fire to be dried out thoroughly. She laid a bare hand on today's top log. Its rough bark was so cold she couldn't tell whether it was damp. Green came off on her skin.

Yellow eyes looked down at her.

Every day, after waking, she had a numb period of not remembering the story so far. Then, somehow, she found herself in her sitting room with the curse cards lined on the mantel where she'd insisted they be displayed... and it all came back. 'Previously... on "Holiday at Six Elms"...'

She shouldn't have stood down the Gargantuabots cadre. They'd done a better job of protection than the possibly ancient doorstep wardstones. As usual, it was all her fault. Silly Little Angie. Mad Old Mum. Witchy Witchy Wickings.

That was one of Janet Speke's – Witchy Witchy Wickings.

The last she'd heard from Janet was after she went Christian. Angie didn't recognise the adult voice on the phone. Janet said, 'I want you to know I've forgiven you,' and hung up before Angie could ask, 'For what?'

Kneeling by the hearth, she teepeed kindling over a firelighter. She poked in paper twists – torn strips of yesterday's envelope. She daren't burn the cards themselves. In an M. R. James story, burning the runes meant losing the last slight chance of evading the curse. Burning an envelope was acceptable nose-thumbing at the Holly Child. Petty defiance.

She found matches and touched flame to the firelighter, relishing the hit of paraffin whiff.

Hugging her knees, she settled back to watch the fire grow. Meagre warmth reached her face.

The envelope strips curled like salted slugs. She piled today's logs into the grate and smelled bark-smoke before they caught. The blaze unfroze her front and hands, though her back stayed icy. She sat closer than parents would advise. If it wasn't googly eyes from the telly it was singed fringe from the fire.

She got up and scanned the room.

The fire fish eye reflected in dangling baubles. The poor old tree was neglected. Its lower branches were yellowing. The tub was cracked. Something like a root poked out a knotted thumb. Earth spilled on the carpet.

The tree must be too close to the fire – though it was in the same place it'd been since Wickingses came to Six Elms. Chocolate Santas and snowmen had melted in their wrappers then set in elongated goop shapes. Jolly Old Saint Nick had soot on his red robe and looked more like Sad Santa. The Wonky Angel hung upside down, ankle caught in a string of dead fairy lights.

She tried to set the Angie Gabrielle right, but realised it'd be a major operation. Involving pliers.

The fire crackled now, almost ferocious, consuming too much wood. A roaring fire, 1850s-style. You could boil a cauldron on it.

Heat haze rose over the mantel. Maybe the blessed cards would burn of their own accord and it would be over.

She thought of doing a Janet and forgiving them.

Then, she remembered Dad singing…

Children roasting on an open fire… Jack Frost ripping off his clothes…

Pained hissing from the logs. A plink – a bauble cracking from heat.

Then, *whump* and an ice-blast enveloped her whole body

like an Arctic airbag. She coughed on smoke.

The fire was out. The updraught had dislodged a plug of snow which fell down the chimney and smothered flame. An ice boulder broke up in the grate.

Without firelight, the room was dim and dingy. She relit the stubs of yesterday's candles.

Something like a shard of mirror flashed in the fireplace. A shining oblong.

A card was propped on the heap of snow-chunks and unburned wood. Silver paper. Classy. Once you got into the twenties, the game was upped. Still the same writing. Number by the stamp. '22'.

Russell came into the room. He'd be wanting his breakfast gruel, growing lad that he be. She waved his card.

'Traditional delivery,' she told him. 'Sleigh on the roof... pressie down the chimney.'

Russell slumped onto the sofa. She plucked the envelope from the heap and dropped it in his lap.

'From the flue to you-hoo-oo...'

Her son contemplated the envelope, too weak to move. He was green about the gills. Poppette would prescribe Milk of Magnesia and warm salt water. Poppette's vile remedies kept Gaffer going into his nineties.

Russell's frozen sausage fingers couldn't work the gummed flap.

She looked along the mantel. The Holly Child was swollen, ready to escape...

'The Cards' owed a lot to 'The Mezzotint', she realised. Had she read that story by 1979? It all went back to M. R. James. Mr Rooke was like the villain of 'Lost Hearts' too. Was her thoughtographed nightmare from beyond time and space a shameless rip-off? Answers on a... on anything but a Christmas card.

Today's card had to be out of its sheath and on the mantel for the curse to progress.

She laughed.

'Here's a howd'ye-do,' she said. 'You've beaten us too soon. Two more chopping days till Christmas and we're done for. We've been got. Got good. Now what?'

A beat like a snare-drum. Logs snapping? Icicles falling?

Russell jerked out of his slump, shoulders hitching, head up. His fingers went into action, tearing the top of the envelope, then squeezing. Like the queen of spades in a magic trick, the card rose of its apparent own accord and opened out four-ways. Not just a panorama, but IMAX 3D. The Holly Child filled a bigger space and was grinning. Nearly time for a goose dinner.

Russell read the card message in a squeaky ventriloquist dummy voice,

TWENTY-TWO, A GIFT FOR YOU...

He was pulled up off the sofa as if by strings and marched to the fireplace. He put the card in position, near the end of the line. Had the mantel stretched over the month? There was always space, though she'd have sworn on December the First there wouldn't be room for twenty-four cards.

The wretched wassailers were readying for a dirty fight with seasonal weapons. Sharpened candy canes, icicle bayonets, bauble bombs, fairy light garottes, antlers.

Russell's strings were cut and he stumbled.

'Mum, what…?'

She looked at the cards – then at her son.

Too little time. Too much to do.

'We've eaten all the mince pies,' she said. 'I'll make more. With too much mince. With so much mince you'll be sick. Won't that be lovely?'

Rust sank back on the sofa, into the rut made long ago by Grandad's bottom. He hadn't enjoyed today's funny turn. He held up his treacherous hands and flexed his fingers. He was in charge again – but cold, exhausted and ill. He hacked as if it were still possible to cough up the seed. He tasted cinnamon.

Someone sat next to him. His neck was too stiff to turn and see her.

He knew who it was – if not what it was. Did it count as an apparition if you didn't look at it.

'You again,' he said.

Which ghost of Christmas was she? Past, Present or Alternate Reality?

Laughing hurt and made him cough.

He felt a small head lean against his arm.

The dusty expanse of the enormoscreen was dull grey. It needed wiping with its special fluid and cloth. It reflected the whole room. The little girl sat beside Rust, hair in bunches. The decorated tree bent over the sofa like a photo-bombing parent. A family portrait.

A white spot in the middle of the screen popped out into an image – not filling the panorama, forming a square like an old television. A bloke in a gold turban and harem pantaloons

KIM NEWMAN

didn't know two heavies with scimitars were creeping up on him, wicked eyes gleaming.

A raucous jangle of children's voices: *Mae e tu ôl i chi!*

Beth? Na... does neb yno! said Aladdin, turning just as the heavies ducked behind pillars. He looked back.

'Look behind you,' said Rust.

Nid yw'n deg, said Aladdin. *Rydych chi'n chwarae triciau arnaf.*

The whole procedure again – look behind you, there's nobody there, look behind you...

Tu ôl i chi! Tu ôl i chi!

Does neb yna!

A pantomime in Welsh. From 1979.

More flashback characters paraded into the sitting room, ignoring whoever was on the sofa.

Nana – younger than Rust remembered – was cross. She silent screamed frustration. Grandad – also youngish – followed her in. Her apron front and some of his face were floury.

Rust never knew Nana and Grandad – Eileen and Frank – when they were together.

'You've upset the child,' said Frank.

Eileen stumped off. Frank did his parrot-face – which Rust remembered – at the children on the sofa. They both obliged him with chuckles. Eileen turned in the doorway and made stabbing motions at her husband's back.

Look behind you...

Frank turned. There was no one there.

Then there was no Frank here.

Rust was alone on the sofa.

At least now he knew why the apparition had his face.

∽

Angie started rolling pastry before she remembered pies wouldn't cook on a camping stove. But she was in a kitchen mood and pressed on with the slapstick routine. They were out of mince pies with too much mince. That must be remedied.

She danced, sprinkling flour. She heard 'Danse des Mirlitons'.

'Everyone's a fruit and nut-caaase... crazy for those mouldy lumps of raisin... every time you eat some, odour from your feet comes... such a stinky pongy stench you'll certainly sick *uhpppp!*'

She flattened lumpy pastry with Mum's old wooden rolling pin. She made herself a witch nose out of dough and stuck it on her face.

She dolloped gobbets of mince into and around pastry cups. Soft pancakey lids fit over messy, overstuffed pies. She skipped edge-crimping. Time to cut snarly faces into the uncooked crusts. In the oven, mince would pop out of eye- and mouth-holes.

She plucked the Norma Bates knife from the magnetic strip.

Norma Bates had it over Harry Kellerman and Tyler Durden. She owned a big knife and knew where to stick it. Norma Bates didn't just write letters. She cut through red tape. And a shower curtain. She got things done.

Of course she did – she was a mother.

Three pies were on the slab. Angie started on the first snarly face.

We three kings of Orient are, bearing gifts shoplifted from Spar.

The nose and mouth slits ran together. The gash was a royal sneer.

'Unfortunately, we're anti-monarchy in this house,' she said.

At first, she stabbed carefully – making multiple pricks. Then, the red mist came down and she shifted to a blitz attack.

'Death to kings! Off with their crowns! Stop your squirmin', ermine vermin!'

Blobs of mince and dough got strewn around. A squirt of fruity juice hit her in the face.

She saw she'd made a terrible mess.

She also saw Russell, standing by the door. Terrified.

She knew what she must look like. Norma Bates in the bathroom.

You've upset the child.

She remembered Dad saying that.

When? Must have been… Christmas. Wickings Christmas wasn't all fun and mischief. It had been a strain, on occasion. A massive strain. Still was, come to think of it.

She put down the knife.

'We've been naughty all year,' she told her son. 'This is what we deserve.'

∽

The next day, Rust stayed in bed, taking a sickie – fully dressed, under two duvets.

He couldn't play games or listen to the Knell of Doom pod or scoff at haunted site explorations on YouTube, so he had to pay attention to the house.

Mum was bustling downstairs. He didn't know which version of her was dominant and was staying out of the way to avoid finding out. What if Mum got got by the Holly Child and left Little Angie behind? Would Rust have to be her parent? One thing, if that happened, he'd enforce strict limits on her screen-viewing time. In bed by nine, and no devices under the duvet.

In the evening, he crept down to forage for food. Not turkey. The sitting room door was open a crack.

Mum sat by the low table, her hair in lopsided bunches. She'd taken Jolly Old Saint Nick and the Wonky Angel down from the tree and was playing with them the way he used to play with G-bots.

She had them talk to each other in high and low voices.

"'Ho Ho Ho,'" she said, deep.

"'That's too much too much mince, Frank,'" she responded, shrill.

"'No such thing as too much too much.'"

"'Stop messing about…'"

Jolly Old Saint Nick jumped up and down, rubbing against the Wonky Angel.

"'Have you been naughty this year, little girl?'"

"'Leave off. This is the tricky bit.'"

"'A tricky bit, eh? A bit tricky for the trickiest of bits… Reach into my sack, little girl…'"

"'Frank. Stop. Angie…'"

'…"You've upset the child.'"

Mum knocked the figures' heads together. She took her hands away to let them fall.

In her own voice, she said, 'This is what happens after Little Angie's bedtime. This is what after-bedtime telly is all about.'

She looked at the door. Rust darted away, which gave him a twinge.

He got to halfway up the stairs and sat down. He needed a rest before he could climb further. Still starving, he felt stuffed.

The sitting room door opened.

Mum was here again, more herself.

'A card came,' she said. 'Mysteriously. Left on the desk. I opened it. Didn't want to wake you. Sorry.'

He couldn't go up or down.

'Poor love,' Mum said. 'What's wrong?'

She was normal – only she shouldn't be. To be normal now meant shutting out most of the last month. Which would be mad.

'Everything,' he said. 'It doesn't make sense.'

She sat on the steps below him and patted his knees.

'I know, love.'

'It's killing Christmas, Mum.'

'Christmas copped it a long time ago. It was never what you remember, the way it is on cards and calendars... robins and crisp snow which doesn't freeze your baps off... an eight-course meal for the whole family, prepared with no effort and presented like a Homepride advert. Wickings Christmas was only slightly for me, for Little Angie... it was for Dad, first, when Mum made the effort... and look where that got him. Then it was for you – lovely and fun and naughty again. Even terrible telly was something to share scorning – a disappointing Doctor Who and celebrities and politicians murdering dance routines when we'd rather they murdered each other. But you've got – what? – maybe one or two more years of giving a shit before you do Christmas just to humour Mad Mum and her mince pies, then find excuses to get out of it. Skiing over the holidays with your uni mates... snow on the railways. Then it's all over. Look at you, Japanese Robot Boy – when you have kids, you won't do any of this. You'll take them to that hotel in Tokyo shaped like Godzilla.'

He'd shown her pictures online. It was tempting...

'Mind you,' she said, 'this Christmas is an all-timer… a *special* special time… and it's only Christmas Eve Eve.'

'What did the card say?'

DECEMBER TWENTY-THIRD, HANG THAT BIRD…

She picked Rust up in her arms and carried him upstairs. She didn't have to strain. He must have lost weight.

'Tell you what – "The Cards" comes from someone who never had to cook Christmas dinner. Leave it till the twenty-third to hang the bird and you're tragically behind schedule.'

She took him to his room and tucked him in bed.

He wasn't hungry any more. She crimped the duvets around him.

'Two more sleeps till Christmas,' she said.

'I'm never sleeping again,' he murmured, eyes shut.

'If this whole experience has taught us one thing, it's the importance of strict bedtimes for children. Night night.'

The busiest day of the year was Christmas Eve.

Angie wore an apron and Santa hat.

She had presents to wrap and kitchen prep to do. The last page of her December checklist was a sub-list of things that must be done by or on the 24th.

In many ways, today was the climax of the season.

The last day of Advent. Hence, twenty-four windows only on that binned calendar. Heretical advent calendars added a double window for Christmas Day. Not the Wickings way.

Her checklist for the 25th had only one item. *Christmas!*

No post on Christmas Day, of course. But they could expect a late surge today. She had a present for Post-Lady Petal.

This year, there were challenges. But no need to give up.

From the kitchen, she heard the Milk Float.

Pa-rum-pa-pum pum Pa-rum-pa-pum pum…

She took Petal's present outside.

∽

Today, Rust could hardly feel anything. His insides were concrete. His skin was ice. It was hard to move.

He sat on the sofa and looked at the mantel.

Every time he swept his gaze across the cards, he saw the Holly Child and the Jingle Basterds marching towards the room. Just one more picture and they'd be here, crowding around the sofa.

The fireplace was a cradle for unburned logs and sooty snow. Without a fire going, the sitting room was as cold as the rest of the house.

He felt warmth in his hand. A friendly grip. Little Angie.

This was not a curse but a paraphenomenon. Curses were a simple-minded way of imposing meaning on a random universe.

But if it waddled like a curse, quacked like a curse… what was it?

He heard the postie come and go. Mum even went outside, through the kitchen door. The weight of the story was too much to resist. She'd bring in the last card and he'd open it. Then they'd get got. Just as well he had no plans for New Year's Eve. He wouldn't even get to play with his big present. Which ought to be wrapped and under the broke-spined tree but wasn't yet. Mum left wrapping till Christmas Eve, because he'd once rattled his under-the-tree present so much to work out what it was that it got broken before it was opened.

Mum came in with a tray. She'd brought out the posh tea service. Raw Christmassy lumps – cake mix with Smarties and sprinkles – were arranged on red-and-green serviettes. A double-sized envelope was propped between teapot and milk-jug. Mum set the elevenses things down on the low table.

She was smarter this morning, even in a Santa hat. Her hair was pinned up. She'd put on lipstick and eyeliner. Her Chef's Kiss apron was clean. Take a picture and this could be a John Lewis ad. Until you noticed the pointy dough nose. She'd stuck a raisin in it as a witch wart.

'Shall I be mother?' she said, brightly.

She'd been saying that before pouring tea from the pot ever since he could remember. If it was a joke, it had never been explained. Of course she was mother. Who else would she be? Nana said the same thing. A phrase of power passed down from mother to daughter? He wasn't included in the secret.

She poured cold water into two cups. She hadn't even put a teabag in.

So, still mental.

He looked at the envelope.

To Master Russell Wickings,
Six Elms House,
nr Sutton Mallet, Somerset.

That same curly writing, twice the size in proportion. The number '24' was bigger too, next to two Christmas stamps. The postmark was Sutton Mallet. The village didn't have a sorting office – anything stuck in the pillar box by the green got franked in the County Town. So this was a special production, just for them.

'Once it's opened, Christmas can really begin,' said Mum.

A small hand on his arm held him back. But he steeled himself. It had to be done. You couldn't spend a week assembling a thousand-piece Gargantuabase Island jigsaw and have the last piece in your hand with the last hole in front of you... and *not* fit it in, even if its action set off the self-destruct system. As in 'Perfidious Puzzle', *Gargantuabots: The Series*, Season Three, Episode Six.

'It'll just be a robin, Mum,' he said. 'Or Santa's sleigh. Or a snowman.'

She handed him his cup and saucer. He sipped – yes, cold water, with a tinny taste – and spat it back. She took a swig and made a big-eyed 'mmm delicious' face. Her Santa pom-pom jingled.

Time to rip off the Elastoplast.

He put his cup down and took the envelope. Using a teaspoon as a letter-opener, he ripped along the top and drew out the bigger, thicker card.

CHRISTMAS EVE, WOULD YOU BELIEVE...

He peeped inside. She was right.

'What's the picture? What's the picture?'

He showed her.

'Oh,' she said, disappointed.

The double-sized card was blank white.

'Polar bear in a snowstorm,' he suggested.

'There'd be eyes. Red eyes.'

He ran his fingers over the card. Was it a printing mistake? Or a secret ink which only appeared when held over a candle?

'Put it with the others,' Mum said.

He got up and walked round the low table.

He looked again at the progression of pictures. A disappointing punchline, though he supposed he should be grateful. While being suspicious. Proper stories had endings. On the last page, you found everything out. It wasn't blank.

He propped the card in the final spot on the mantelpiece.

It unfolded – more white, but twice the size… then unfolded again, four times as big… taking up all the mantel-space, swinging down over the fireplace like a fireguard… and again, making a new, fresh wall… a white expanse, swirling… silkily semi-transparent so you could see the cut logs and sooty snow beyond the veil.

There were eyes. Red eyes.

And black vertical stripes. Trees.

Rust fell to his knees, ripped apart by pain, and pitched forward – through whiteness into the hearth. He squirmed onto his back.

He wasn't looking up through a chimney. Above was a curve of night sky. No moon, just a red star.

Wind whipsawed through woods. The Holly Child and the Merciless Gentlemen were out there. He glimpsed the Jingle Basterds, nipping between trees, taking cover out of his sightline.

Bells rung somewhere near.

He tried to fight the pains shifting inside him. He gripped snow with his bare hands. His fingers scraped hard earth.

'There now,' said Mum. 'Let it grow, let it grow, let it grow…'

She had stepped through the hearth – a portal – after him.

The winter woodland hadn't been swarming out to get

143

them – but expanding to suck them in. This was what being got was like. Inside an infinite snow globe.

Mum was comfortable here in the cold and dark. Her nose wasn't dough any more, but grown from her actual face.

Cinnamon spew welled up in his gullet. He swallowed it.

His hands were creaky wooden soldier paws. He tried to stand.

'A perfect Christmas scene,' said Mum.

They weren't in the sitting room any more. This was in the cards – in the world of the cards… a Narnia-in-winter horror forest… the abode of the stoats and weasels and witchy witchy witches… eternal night before Christmas. Dreamed by Little Angie, lived by all the Wickingses. Someone should have given his mother more than a lump of coal. This was the world according to Mr Rooke from 'The Cards'.

They were the toys of the Joy Leech, who'd break them by Boxing Day.

All around were naturally decorated Christmas trees – bauble fruit dangling, wrapped present puffballs in the roots, robins in cage-nests, rat-santas scurrying in the upper branches, skirmishing with wasp-angels.

His mother was silhouetted against a white oblong. The portal from there to here. Six Elms lay back beyond the mist.

'It's a tesseract,' he said, 'a private pocket universe defined by our unconscious… not just yours, but mine, and other people's…'

'An explanation! You take the fun out of everything.'

Something else barged through the portal. A walking fir tree. The Holly Child, all grown-up – and bent to spite and malice. A promise of a cold, cruel Christmas. It was here with its people.

'You're the real joy leech, Russell,' said Mum. 'In a season of giving, you take take take…'

She wasn't her, really. She was her worst her.

Witchy Witchy Wickings.

'So you didn't get the right gargantuablaster six years ago… you got something just as good.'

He'd forgotten that. She got him a Series Three Blaster, which wasn't compatible with his Series Two Gargantuastrikeforce.

'Remember what you got me for Christmas that year? Do you remember anything you've ever given me… because I can't. Anything there? Or is it just blank?'

That wasn't fair. He'd filled her *Fontana Book of Great Ghost Stories* gaps this year. Books didn't really count, though. He noticed everyone else gave Mum books – she was a writer, so she must need more books – so he tried hard to find other presents for her. Her big present from him this year was a murder mystery board game they could play together. He'd already made a start on learning the rules. When the videopod earnings came in, he was going to buy her a chainsaw for her next birthday so they could retire the axes. He knew she'd love a dangerous power tool. She chopped to take her mind off plot problems. Chainsawing would be much more satisfying.

The Holly Child had fetched the big axe. He handed it to Mum.

She took a few swings.

It was a small mercy he'd gone with the murder mystery board game this Christmas and put the chainsaw off till her next birthday.

Time to play hide and seek at the highest difficulty level.

Ignoring the twisting in his stomach, he ran into the woods.

'Ho ho ho,' howled someone behind him. Not the Swine of Sedgemoor.

His tracks in the snow would be easy to follow. He dodged around trees, hoping to throw some confusion in his trail.

He ran and ran, deeper into the dark woods. His chest hurt from inhaling ice-drops. Damn alveoli again.

He got a stitch – so bad he thought he'd brushed a scythe-blade and opened his side.

He stopped running and doubled over. Here was where he'd get got good. In this spot between tall trees – inside a thoughtographed snow globe, whipped up by desires and dreads formed years before he was born, given shape by primal forces in the environs of the most haunted village in England. Peasons in a Pod would do a series about his disappearance and get famous.

A hand pinched his sleeve.

He shrivelled with terror, but it was the girl. The ghost of Little Angie from 1979. Strictly, if the original person were still alive, the apparition was not a ghost but a fetch. A doppelganger was when the apparition was an identical twin. A fetch was if the shade was who the person used to be or has yet to become.

He was older than this version of his mother, but she looked after him.

She pulled him into a hollow tree, which was a snug fit. And out of sight.

He peeped through a knothole. A hunting party of wooden soldiers was out. The redcoat squaddies weren't happy drawing this detail over the holidays. They'd rather be in a warm tavern with ale and strumpets. Little Angie covered his mouth so the Jingle Basterds wouldn't hear him breathe and cough. Her hand was spicy, as if she'd been cooking.

'Mum,' he whispered, 'this is not your fault.'

A wooden corporal had the bright idea of bayonetting random trees. His mates started stabbing.

Time to quit this cosy nook and flee.

He had his second wind. Stitch was almost gone.

He held Little Angie's hand and gave a three-two-one countdown. They broke out, getting up speed, weaving between trees. Not being wooden, they were nippier on their feet. The soldiers kept head-butting trunks… pine needles showered them like shrapnel… bauble bombs went off.

They were on a path rimmed with fairy lights, like a winding runway.

Up ahead was an open-fronted stable, lit by six-foot candles. Giant stuffed rats in Middle Eastern robes posed as Joseph and Mary. Two crowned weasels and a badger bore gifts. Kaspar, Melchior and the Other One. The Nativity Mob's clothes were held together by big stitches. Other embalmed animals – giant shrews and mice – represented shepherds and, disturbingly, sheep. All gathered around a manger. Rust knew a manger was a trough animals ate out of and therefore actually a really stupid thing to use as a crib… especially in bleak midwinter with hay running low and shrew-toothed sheep pretty much up to chew on anything.

This was from 'The Cards'. Mum had remembered it.

Rust and Little Angie walked hand in hand to the Nativity Scene.

In the manger was a big pink slug with wriggling horns.

Slime Baby Jesus.

Little Angie cooed in adoration. Mum loved slugs and snails

and creepy things. Rust was less keen, especially if they were the wrong size.

If this tesseract was inside her head, he wouldn't like to live here.

Little Angie liked the slime baby but thought one particular shrew-sheep had its glass eye on her and malice in its sawdust-stuffed heart. She clung to him. He remembered all the times he'd had nightmares and woken his mum. She'd made it better by being silly and kind, turning frightening things he dreamed up into jokes they could mock together.

It was his fault, he thought. For not believing hard enough. For being selfish and ungrateful, unappreciative of effort and sacrifice. He'd heard that song before. He bet Mum had too, from Grandad and Nana. This place wasn't just Angie Little or Tall – it was him too… and Frank (a lot) and Eileen (a little), and Gaffer and what-was-her-name from before his time. And a general free-floating sense of the seamier side of the season.

This was what Wickings Christmas grew up to be.

He admitted it. This was the Christmas present he deserved. A lump of coal.

The stable was surrounded now. The Holly Child and the Jingle Basterds were here.

Only one person was giving orders. Witchy Witchy Wickings.

Mum walked into the Nativity. Little Angie hid behind Rust – afraid of who she'd be in years to come. Mum had her Santa hat and big axe.

The sky was red now. That bloody star.

'It's the *effort*,' said Mum, on one of her rants, 'the ingratitude, the tidying, the pine needles, the shaming, the smugness. Sour sweets, broken bulbs, wrong connector cords, wrong presents, wrong everything. And fucking "Fairytale of New York". I hate that song. Your nana, my mum, once spent seventeen hours in the kitchen preparing an umpteen-course meal only for Poppette, my nana, to sniff her slice of Christmas pudding and whine, "Where's the brandy butter?" Mum had provided two types of cream, but – oh no – without sodding brandy butter, she might as well have ordered the whole lot from McDonald's. That's *Christmas*, Russell Rusty Rust. Ho Ho Ho.'

'This isn't you, Mum,' Rust said.

She was taken aback. 'Has that *ever* worked as an argument? "This isn't you." Said to a her who manifestly is her? A me secure in my me-ness?'

'*This* is you, Mum,' said Rust.

He put his hands on Little Angie's shoulders.

Mum looked down at her own face. They matched except for the nose. And the bunches.

The Merciless Gentlemen pressed in, muttering in the ranks. They were here for blood and fire and hot toddies afterwards.

'This is the original you, Mum. The you who started telling stories.'

Mum took off her dough nose and threw it to the slime baby.

'Look at those bell-ropes,' said Mum, tugging fondly on one of Little Angie's bunches. 'They never matched. Janet Speke used to call me "Wonky Weirdie" before she hit on "Witchy Witchy". She had a thing for alliteration before me. Goat's sake, I've just realised I copied it from her.'

Mum gave Little Angie's bunch an encouraging shake.

'It's not a mystery story,' she told herself, 'not a horror story… it's a ghost story… a miracle story… a *Christmas* story.'

She hugged the child and took her into her heart.

There was only one Angie here now. Mum, but with bunches. She shook her head and they came loose.

Rust coughed. Mum thumped his back. He spat up the foul chocolate seed, which had shrivelled back into itself.

The Holly Child was just a tree. The Jingle Basterds were tiny ornaments hung from branches – soldiers, santas, snowmen. A robin warbled, up top where the angel should be. The Merciless Gentlemen were back in their boxes. They could go on eBay or under the stairs.

Behind Mum was the veiled portal.

Her son took her hand and walked her through the fireplace back into the sitting room. They didn't bump their heads.

On the mantel were only dried flakes. Like the crumbled pages of a poorly preserved old book. Barely a dustpan's worth.

'Uck,' she said. 'Mess.'

There were pine needles all over the carpet. Fillip's bowl was turned over. She hadn't put presents under the tree yet.

Oh, and the power was still cut.

Merry As Per Usual.

Russell found Jolly Old Saint Nick and the Wonky Angel on the low table. They'd had a hard time of it, lately – but you had to love them just the same. They did their best by their lights.

'Put those back in their proper places,' she told Russell.

He snapped to, obedient child – and put the Christmas couple up on the tree. A few branches down, miniature Angie and Rust – survivors of the mailbox massacre – huddled in a clump of dates.

Fairy lights came on and other devices throughout the house. They'd tried to remember what was switched on when the power went off but could only make guesses. Now they'd know.

From the digital radio in the kitchen came a children's choir singing 'Once in Royal David's City' in Welsh.

She hugged her son and he didn't struggle.

He would soon – she had, she remembered – but he'd grow up and get over being embarrassed by public affection and want to hug back, more and more as it sank in that she wouldn't be here for infinite Christmases yet to come. That sweet thought went dark quickly. She really ought to watch out for that.

'I'm sorry, Russell.'

'Rust,' he corrected.

'Rust.'

The kitchen was an unholy mess. Little was remotely edible. The fridge light came on again. The radiators were warming up. The timer would be jiggered and it'd be an hour's session with the manuals and YouTube tutorials to get it sorted out.

According to Horst's digital watch, it was 12.03.

'Merry Christmas, Rust,' she said.

'Merry Christmas, Mum.'

He found a Tesco bag to wrap the turkey corpse in, so it could be properly disposed of. That menu was scotched.

'So,' she said, 'how about "Christmas Day... Chinese takeaway"?'

> '... and now, not for viewers of a nervous
> disposition or children who should be in
> their beds, we repeat a classic from the
> archives... first broadcast in 1979...'
>
>   A CHRISTMAS GHOST STORY
>   (Stori Ysbryd Nadolig)

'*THE CARDS*'
(Y Cardiau)

A bleak December landscape. The snow cover
isn't soft delight...

... twenty-three cards in a row.

Rooke is bloated to bursting in his lair,
lulled by a surfeit of stolen joy. The skeleton-
winged robin flies out of the card and pecks
at his eye, which is a big glass bauble.

Master Christimas, you've not beat me yet...

Twigs poke out of his neck, ripping through
flesh. His robe splits open in half a dozen
places. The buboes on his chest hatch into
decorations - stars, humbugs, bells.

A tree-branch hand presents him with the final
card, marked '24'. He takes it.

Christimas Eve - pah! I'm not afraid of you...

He opens the card and the Holly Child inside
pokes out through his flesh. Rooke's head is
speared on the tip of the tree. He looks down
and sees red scraps of his skin decorating the
dark branches. Bells jingle.

The tree grows through the roof of Wychward
Cottage and spreads into the skies.

Rooke's side-whiskers catch light and his
head rises from the treetop like a rocket,
streaking across the sky above Rokesby
Roylott. A shooting star.

Villagers stir, puzzled at their momentary darkness of mood. Merriment flowers. Smiles return. Goodwill blossoms.

Villagers wish each other compliments of the season, shake hands, embrace. Beadle Bramblebush and the Fimples are jolly again. Children scamper in the snow, eager to play with their presents. The choir reassembles. The Reverend Godly takes up his baton. In harmony, they sing...

Joy to the world! The Lord is come;
Let Earth receive her King;
Let every heart prepare him room
And heaven and nature sing,
And heaven and nature sing,
And heaven, and heaven, and nature sing.

The flaming star explodes. Fragments fall as glittering snow.

ACKNOWLEDGEMENTS

Thanks to Prano Bailey-Bond, Dan Berlinka, Eugene Byrne, Susan Byrne, Robert Chandler, Simret Cheema-Innis, Meg Davis, Alex Dunn, Barry Forshaw, Mark Gatiss, Neil Gaiman, Sean Hogan, Rod Jones, Stephen Jones, Julia Lloyd, Paul McAuley, Maura McHugh, Adrian McLaughlin, Helen Mullane, Louise Pearce, Claire Schultz, Paul Simpson, Brian Smedley and Cath Trechman. Thanks also to my family, who managed a fifty-year stretch of traditional Christmases in Somerset − Bryan and Julia Newman (who did let me watch those ghost stories in the 1970s), Sasha and Jerome Newman, and my grandmother Miranda who was particular about brandy butter.

ABOUT THE AUTHOR

KIM NEWMAN is an award-winning writer, critic, journalist and broadcaster who lives in London. He is a contributing editor to the UK film magazine *Empire*, and writes its popular monthly segment, 'The Cult of Kim Newman'. He also writes for assorted publications including *Sight & Sound*, *The Dark Side* and *The Guardian*. He makes frequent appearances on radio and TV, and is the chief writer of the BBC TV series *Mark Kermode's Secrets of Cinema*.

He has won many awards, including the Bram Stoker®, International Horror Guild, Prix Ozone, British Fantasy, and British Science Fiction Awards, and been nominated for the Hugo, World Fantasy and James Herbert Awards. Kim also writes non-fiction books focused on popular culture, film and television, including a comprehensive overview of the horror film industry, *Nightmare Movies* (Bloomsbury).

You can keep up to date with Kim's events and writing via his website johnnyalucard.com. Find him on social media @annodracula.

For more fantastic fiction, author events,
exclusive excerpts, competitions, limited editions and more

VISIT OUR WEBSITE
titanbooks.com

LIKE US ON FACEBOOK
facebook.com/titanbooks

FOLLOW US ON TWITTER AND INSTAGRAM
@TitanBooks

EMAIL US
readerfeedback@titanemail.com